TALOS CLAIMS HIS VIRGIN

BY

MICHELLE SMART

MILLS &
BOON®

First published in Great Britain 2015
By Mills & Boon, an imprint of HarperCollins*Publishers*
1 London Bridge Street, London, SE1 9GF

Large Print edition 2016

© 2015 Michelle Smart

ISBN: 978-0-263-26177-6

Printed and bound in Great Britain
by CPI Antony Rowe, Chippenham, Wiltshire

*This book is dedicated to Amalie,
who's been on this journey with me
every step of the way. xxx*

CHAPTER ONE

TALOS KALLIAKIS DIPPED his head and rubbed the nape of his neck. The consultant's words had cut through to his marrow.

Looking back up to stare at his two brothers, he read the sorrow on their faces.

Astraeus Kalliakis—the King of Agon, their grandfather—was dying.

Helios, the eldest of the three brothers and heir to the throne, folded his arms and took a visible deep breath before breaking the silence. 'We need to bring the Jubilee celebrations forward.'

The whole of Agon was gearing up to celebrate Astraeus's fifty years on the throne. Everything was planned for the end of summer, six months away. The consultant oncologist had said in no uncertain terms he wouldn't last that long.

Talos cleared his throat before speaking. His vocal cords had never felt so raw. 'I suggest we concentrate on the Jubilee Gala and cancel the rest of the celebrations—they're all superfluous. Let's make the gala a true celebration of his life.'

'Agreed,' said Theseus, the middle brother, nodding. 'We should set the date for April—three months from now. It will be a push, but between us and the courtiers we can do it and do it well.'

Any later and there was every possibility their grandfather would not be there for it. Two months of intense chemotherapy would buy him time and shrink the tumours riddling his organs. But they would not cure him. It was too late for that.

Two months later

Talos Kalliakis headed through the back of the theatre that housed the Orchestre National de Paris, noting the faded, peeling wallpaper, the threadbare carpet that had to be older than his thirty-three years, the water-stained ceiling... No wonder the building was on the verge of being condemned. Of all the orchestral homes he'd visited in the past two months, the facilities here were by far the worst.

But he wasn't here for the facilities. He'd come here on a whim, when he'd been left disappointed by the violinists from all of France's other major orchestras, as he'd been left underwhelmed by those from the major orchestras of Greece, Italy, Spain and England.

Time was running out.

What he had assumed would be a simple task had turned into a marathon of endurance.

All he wanted to find was that one special musician, someone who could stroke a bow over the bridge of their violin and make his heart soar the way his grandmother had when she'd been alive. He would never claim to have a musical ear, but he was certain that when he heard it he would know.

The chosen violinist would be rewarded with the honour of playing his grandmother's final composition, accompanied by his or her own orchestra, at his grandfather's Jubilee Gala.

At that moment approximately a dozen Orchestre National de Paris violinists were lining up, ready to audition for him.

He just wanted it to be over.

The weak, impatient part of himself told him to settle on *anyone*. Everyone who had auditioned for him thus far had been professional, note-perfect, the sounds coming from their wooden instruments a delight to anyone's ear. But they hadn't been a delight to his heart, and for once in his life he knew he had to select the right person based on his heart, not his head.

For his grandfather's Jubilee Gala he wouldn't—couldn't—accept anything or anyone but the best. His grandfather deserved no less. His grandmother's memory deserved no less.

Flanked by the orchestra directors, an assistant and his own translator, they turned single file down a particularly narrow corridor. It was like being in an indoor, dank version of the glorious maze in the Agon palace gardens.

The violinists were lined up backstage; the rest of the musicians sat in the auditorium. He would already be seated at the front of the auditorium himself if roadworks hadn't forced his driver to detour to the back of the theatre rather than drop him at the front.

His mind filled with the dozen other things he needed to be getting on with that he'd had to let slip these past two months. A qualified lawyer, he oversaw all sales, mergers and buyouts with regard to the business empire he'd forged with his two brothers. He didn't *always* use his legal skills to get his own way.

Theseus, the middle Kalliakis brother, had identified an internet start-up seeking investment. If projections were correct, they would quadruple their investment in less than two months. Talos, though, had suspicions about the owners…

His thoughts about unscrupulous techies were cut away when a faint sound drifted out of a door to his left.

He paused, raising a hand in a request for silence.

His ears strained and he rested his head against the door.

There it was.

The only piece of classical music he knew by name.

A lump formed in his throat—a lump that grew with each passing beat.

Wanting to hear more clearly, but not wanting to disturb the violinist, he turned the handle carefully and pressed the door open.

An inch was enough to bring the solemn yet haunting music to life.

His chest filled, bittersweet memories engulfing him.

He'd been seven years old when his parents had died. The nights that had followed, before his brothers had been flown back from their English boarding school—he'd been only a year away from joining them there—had left him inconsolable.

Queen Rhea Kalliakis, the grandmother he'd adored, had soothed him the only way she knew how. She'd come into his room, sat on the edge of his bed and played the 'Méditation' from Jules Massenet's *Thaïs*.

He hadn't thought about this particular piece of music for over twenty-five years.

The tempo was different from the way his grandmother had played it, slower, but the effect was the same. Painful and yet soothing, like balm on a wound, seeping through his skin to heal him from the inside out.

This one had it—the special, elusive *it*.

'That is the one,' he said, addressing the orchestra directors collectively. His translator made the translation in French for them.

The sharp-faced woman to his left looked at him with a searching expression, as if judging whether he was serious, until her eyes lit up and, in her excitement, she flung the door open.

There, in the corner of the room, her violin still under her chin but her bow flailing in her right hand, stood a tall, lithe girl—woman. She had the distinct look of a rabbit caught in the headlights of a speeding car.

* * *

It was those eyes.

She had never seen anything like them before, nor such intensity.

The way they had fixed on her... Like lasers. Trapping her.

Amalie shivered to think of them.

She shivered again when she stepped out of the theatre exit and into the slushy car park. Keeping a firm grip on her violin case—she really needed to get the strap fixed—she tugged her red-and-grey striped beanie hat over her ears.

A long black car with darkened windows entered the car park and crunched its way through the snow to pull up beside her.

The back door opened and a giant got out.

It took a beat before her brain comprehended that it wasn't a giant but Talos Kalliakis.

Intense, striking eyes—were they brown?—fixed on her for the second time in an hour. The effect was as terrifying and giddying the second time around. More so.

When the door of the practice room had swung open and she'd seen all those faces staring at her she'd wanted to shrink into a corner. She hadn't signed up for the audition, but had been told to attend in case the orchestra as a whole was needed. She'd happily hidden away from the action in the room behind the auditorium; there, but not actually present.

Those eyes…

They had rested on her for so long she'd felt as if she'd been stuck in a time capsule. Then they had moved from her face and, without a *bonjour* or *au revoir*, he'd disappeared.

There hadn't been time for her to appreciate the sheer size of the man.

She was tall for a woman—five foot eight. But Talos towered over her, a mass of height and muscle that not even his winter attire could hide.

Her mouth ran dry.

He wore his thick ebony hair slightly too long, messy at the front and curling over the collar of his long black trench coat. Dark stubble, also thick, abounded over his square jawline.

Despite the expensive cut of his clothing, right down to what were clearly handmade shoes, he had a feral air about him, as if he should be swinging through vines in a jungle whilst simultaneously banging his chest.

He looked dangerous. Wildly dangerous. The

scar on his right eyebrow, which seemed to divide it into two, only added to this sense.

He also looked full of purpose.

He took the few steps towards her with long strides, an outstretched hand and an unsmiling face. 'Amalie Cartwright, it is a pleasure to meet you,' he said in perfect English.

How did he know she was bilingual?

God but the man was *enormous*. He had to be a good six and a half feet. Easily.

Swallowing frantically to moisten her mouth, Amalie switched her violin case to her left hand and extended her right to him. It was immediately engulfed in his strong, darkly bronzed hand. It was like being consumed by a giant paw. Even through the wool of her gloves she could feel the heat from his uncovered hand.

'Monsieur Kalliakis,' she murmured in response.

She tugged her hand free and hugged it around her violin case.

'I require your attention. Please, get in the car,' he said.

I require your attention? If she hadn't been so unsettled by him and the deepness of his voice—a low bass both throaty and rich that matched his appearance perfectly—she would have been tempted to laugh at his formality.

With a start she remembered he was a prince. Royalty. Should she curtsey or something? He'd disappeared from the practice room before they could be formally introduced.

She cleared her throat and took a tiny step back. 'My apologies, *monsieur*, but I don't believe there is anything for us to discuss.'

'I assure you there is. Get in the car. It is too cold to have this discussion out here.'

He spoke as only a man used to throwing his weight around could.

'Is this about the solo? I did explain to your assistant earlier that I have a prior engagement for the gala weekend and won't be able to attend. My apologies if the message never reached you.'

The assistant, a middle-aged man with an air of implacability about him, had been unable to hide his shock when she'd said she couldn't do it. The orchestra directors had simply stared at her with pleading eyes.

'The message did reach me—which is why I turned back from the airport and returned here, so I could discuss the matter with you directly.'

His displeasure was obvious, as if it were *her* fault his plans had been ruined.

'You will need to cancel your engagement. I wish for you to play at my grandfather's gala.'

'I wish I could as well,' she lied. A lifetime of dealing with forceful personalities had prepared her well for this moment. No personality came more forceful than her mother's. 'But, no. It is not something I can get out of.'

His brow furrowed in the manner of someone who had never had the word *no* uttered within his earshot. 'You *do* realise who my grandfather is and what a huge opportunity this is for your career?'

'Yes, he is the King of Agon—and I do understand what a great honour it is to be selected to play for him—'

'*And* the majority of the world's great statesmen who will be there—'

'But there are many other violinists in this orchestra,' she continued, speaking over him as if he had not just interrupted. 'If you audition them, as you had planned, you will find most are far more talented than me.'

Of *course* she knew what a huge event the gala was going to be. Her fellow musicians had spoken about little else for weeks. Every orchestra in Europe had been alerted to the fact that Prince Talos Kalliakis was searching for a solo violinist. When it had been confirmed yesterday that he was coming to audition the violinists at the Orchestre National de Paris there had been an immediate mass exodus as every female musician in the orchestra had headed to Paris's beauty parlours for highlights and waxing and all other manner of preening.

The three Princes of Agon were considered Europe's most eligible bachelors. *And* the most handsome.

Amalie had known she wouldn't audition, so hadn't bothered to join the exodus.

If she'd known for a second that Talos had been listening at the door to her practice she would have hit as many bum notes as she could without sounding like a screeching cat.

There was no way—*no way in the world*—she could stand on the stage at the Jubilee Gala and play for the world. No way. She couldn't. The mere thought of it was enough to bring her out in a cold sweat.

The chill of the wind was picking up. She scrunched her toes inside her cold boots, which were getting wetter by the second as the icy snow seeped through the tiny seams and spread to her socks. The back of Talos's car looked very snug and warm. Not that she would find out for herself. The chill in his eyes perfectly matched the weather whipping around them.

'Excuse me, *monsieur*, but I need to go home. We have a concert tonight and I have to be back here in a few hours. Good luck finding your soloist.'

The hardness of his features softened by the slightest of margins, but his eyes—she'd been right, they *were* brown: a light, almost transparent brown, with the blackest of rims—remained hard.

'We will talk again on Monday, *despinis*. Until then I suggest you think hard about what you are giving up by refusing to take the solo.'

'Monday is our day off. I will be in on Tuesday, if you wish to speak to me then, but there will be nothing for us to talk about.'

He inclined his head. 'We shall see. Oh—and when we next meet you may address me by my formal title: Your Highness.'

This time her lips tugged into a smile—one she had no control over. 'But, *monsieur*, this is France. A republic. Even when we had a royal family, male heirs to the throne were addressed by the title of "Monsieur", so I am addressing you correctly. And I feel I should remind you of what happened to those who boasted of having royal blood—they had their heads chopped off.'

Amalie took her seat on the stage, in the second row from the back, nicely encased amongst the orchestra's other second violins. Exactly where she liked to be. Hidden from the spotlight.

While she waited for Sebastien Cassel, their guest conductor, to make his indication for them to start she felt a prickling on her skin.

Casting her eyes out into the auditorium, she saw the projected ticket sales had been correct. She doubted they were even at half capacity.

How much longer could this go on?

Paris was a city of culture. It had accommodated and celebrated its orchestras for centuries. But the other orchestras weren't housed in a flea pit like the Théâtre de la Musique; a glorified music hall. Once, it had been full of pomp and glory. Years of neglect and underinvestment had left it teetering perilously, almost into the red.

A large figure in the stalls to her right, in the most expensive seats in the house, made her blink and look twice. Even as she squinted to focus more clearly the thumping of her heart told her who the figure was and explained the prickling sensation on her skin.

Immediately her thoughts flickered to Prince Talos. There was something about that man and the danger he exuded that made her want to run faster than if a thousand spotlights had been aimed at her. His breathtaking physical power, that gorgeous face with the scar slashing through the eyebrow, the voice that had made her blood thicken into treacle...

Juliette, the violinist she sat next to, dug a sharp elbow into her side.

Sebastien was peering at them, his baton raised.

Amalie forced her eyes to the score before her and positioned herself, praying for her fingers to work.

Being at the back of the eighty-strong number of musicians usually made her feel invisible—just another head in the crowd, with the spotlight well and truly away from her. She couldn't bear having the spotlight pointed at her, had actively avoided it since the age of twelve. More than that: she had cowered from it.

She couldn't see him clearly—indeed, she didn't even know for certain that it *was* him sitting in the stalls—but she couldn't shake the feeling that someone in the audience had their eyes fixed firmly on *her*.

Talos watched the evening unfold. The orchestra was a professional unit and played with a panache even the most musically illiterate could appreciate.

But he wasn't there to listen.

Once the concert had finished he had a meeting with the owner of this ramshackle building.

He'd originally planned to take his jet back to Agon and visit his grandfather, relieved that his two-month search for a violinist was over. Amalie Cartwright's belligerence had put paid to that.

Looking at her now, the fingers of her left hand flying over the strings of her violin, he could not believe her rudeness. Her thin, pretty face, with a sprinkling of freckles over the bridge of her straight nose, gave the illusion of someone dainty, fragile, an image compounded by a form so slender one could be forgiven for worrying about her being blown over in a breeze. She had the elegance so many Parisian women came by with seemingly no effort. He'd seen that earlier, even when her rich brown hair had been hidden under the hat she'd worn to keep the chill in the air at bay.

But looks could be deceiving.

She'd dismissed performing the solo at his grandfather's gala and, by extension, had insulted the Kalliakis name. And her jibe about the French royal family having their heads removed had been a step too far.

Amalie Cartwright *would* take the solo. He would make sure of it.

And what Talos Kalliakis wanted, he got. Always.

CHAPTER TWO

AMALIE BURIED HER HEAD under the pillow and ignored the ringing of her doorbell. She wasn't expecting any visitors or a delivery. Her French mother wouldn't dream of turning up unannounced so early in the morning—anything earlier than midday she considered to be the middle of the night—and her English father was on tour in South America. Whoever it was could come back another time.

Whoever it was clearly had no intention of coming back another time.

The ringing continued, now accompanied by the banging of fists.

Cursing in English and French, she scrambled out of bed, shrugged a thick robe over her pyjama-clad body and, still cursing, hurried down the stairs to open the front door.

'Good morning, *despinis.*'

And with those words Talos Kalliakis brushed past her and entered her home.

'What the…? Excuse me—you can't just let yourself in,' she said, rushing after him while he swept through her narrow house as if he owned it.

'I told you I would be speaking with you today.'

His tone was neutral, as if he were oblivious to her natural shock and anger.

'And I told *you* this is my day off. I would like you to leave.'

He stepped into the kitchen. 'After we have spoken.'

To reiterate his point he set his briefcase on the floor, removed his long black trench coat, which he placed on the back of a chair at her small kitchen table, and sat himself down.

'What are you doing? I didn't invite you in— if you want to speak to me you will have to wait until tomorrow.'

He waved a dismissive hand. 'I will take ten minutes of your time and then I will leave. What we need to discuss will not take long.'

Amalie bit into her cheek and forced her mind to calm. Panicked thinking would not help. 'This is my home and you are trespassing. Leave now or I will call the police.'

He didn't need to know that her mobile phone was currently atop her bedside table.

'Call them.' He shrugged his huge shoulders, the linen of his black shirt rippling with the movement. 'By the time they get here we will have concluded our conversation.'

She eyed him warily, afraid to blink, and rubbed her hands up her arms, backing away, trapping herself against the wall. What could she use as a weapon?

This man was a stranger and the most physically imposing man she had met in her life. The scar that slashed through his eyebrow only compounded the danger he oozed. If he were to…

She wouldn't be able to defend herself using her own strength. It would be like a field mouse fighting a panther.

His top lip curved with distaste. 'You have no need to worry for your safety—I am not an animal. I am here to talk, not to assault you.'

Would the panther *tell* the field mouse he intended to eat her? Of course not. He would insist it was the last thing on his mind and then, when the little field mouse got close enough…*snap!*

Staring into his striking eyes, she saw that, although cold, they contained no threat. A tiny fraction of her fear vanished.

This man would not harm her. Not physically, at any rate.

She dropped her gaze and rubbed her eyes, which had become sore from all that non-blinking.

'Okay. Ten minutes. But you should have called first. You didn't have to barge your way into my home when I was still sleeping.'

An awareness crept through her bones. While he was freshly showered, shaved—minimal stubble today—and dressed, *she* was in old cotton pyjamas and a dressing gown, and suffering from a severe case of bed hair. Talk about putting her at an immediate disadvantage.

He looked at his watch. 'It is ten a.m. A reasonable time to call on someone on a Monday morning.'

To her utter mortification, she could feel her skin heat. It might not be his problem that she'd had hardly any sleep, but it was certainly his fault.

No matter how hard she'd tried to block him from her mind, every time she'd closed her eyes his face had swum into her vision. Two nights of his arrogant face—there, right behind her eyelids. His arrogant, *handsome* face. Shockingly, devilishly handsome.

'This is my day off, *monsieur*. How I choose to

spend it is my business.' Her mouth had run so dry her words came out as a croak. 'I need a coffee.'

'I take mine black.'

She didn't answer, just stepped to the other side of the kitchen and pressed the button on the coffee machine she had set before she went to bed. It kicked into action.

'Have you thought any more about the solo?' he asked as she removed two mugs from the mug tree.

'I told you—there's nothing for me to think about. I'm busy that weekend.' She heaped a spoonful of sugar into one of the mugs.

'I was afraid that would be your answer.'

His tone was akin to a teacher disappointed with his star pupil's exam results. Something about his tone made the hairs on her arms rise in warning.

Water started to drip through the filter and into the pot, drip by hot drip, the aroma of fresh coffee filling the air.

'I am going to appeal to your better nature,' Talos said, staring at Amalie, whose attention was still held by the slowly falling coffee.

She turned her head a touch. 'Oh?'

'My grandmother was a composer and musician.' A short pause. 'Rhea Kalliakis...'

'You have heard of her?'

'I doubt there's a violinist alive who hasn't. She composed the most beautiful pieces.'

A sharp pang ran through him to know that this woman appreciated his grandmother's talents. Amalie couldn't know it, but her simple appreciation only served to harden his resolve that she was the perfect musician for the role. She was the *only* musician.

'She completed her final composition two days before her death.'

She turned from the coffee pot to face him.

Amalie Cartwright had the most beautiful almond-shaped eyes, he noted, not for the first time. The colour reminded him of the green sapphire ring his mother had worn.

That ring now lay in the Agon palace safe, where it had rested for the past twenty-six years, waiting for the day when Helios selected a suitable bride to take guardianship of it. After their grandfather's diagnosis, that day would be coming much sooner than Helios had wanted or expected. Helios needed to marry and produce an heir.

The last time Talos had seen the ring his mother had been fighting off his father. Two hours later the pair of them had been dead.

He cast his mind away from that cataclysmic

night and back to the present. Back to Amalie Cartwright—the one person who could do justice to Rhea Kalliakis's final composition and with it, bring comfort to a dying man. A dying *king*.

'Is that the piece you wish to have played at your grandfather's gala?'

'Yes. In the five years since her death we have kept the score secure and allowed no one to play it. Now we—my brothers and I—believe it is the right time for the world to hear it. And at what better occasion than my grandfather's Jubilee Gala? I believe *you* are the person to play it.'

He deliberately made no mention of his grandfather's diagnosis. No news of his condition had been released to the public at large and nor would it be until after the gala—by decree from King Astraeus, his grandfather, himself.

Amalie poured the freshly brewed coffee into the mugs, added milk to her own, then brought them to the table and took the seat opposite him.

'I think it is a wonderful thing you are doing,' she said, speaking in measured tones. 'There isn't another violinist alive who wouldn't be honoured to be called upon to do it. But I am sorry, *monsieur*, that person cannot be me.'

'Why not?'

'I told you. I have a prior engagement.'

He fixed her with his stare. 'I will double the appearance fee. Twenty thousand euros.'

'No.'

'Fifty thousand. And that's my final offer.'

'No.'

Talos knew his stare could be intimidating, more so than his sheer physicality. He'd performed this stare numerous times in front of a mirror, looking to see what it was that others saw, but had never recognised what it might be. Whatever it was, one throw of that look was enough to ensure he got his own way. The only people immune to it were his brothers and grandparents. Indeed, whenever his grandmother had seen him 'pull that face', as she had referred to it, she'd clipped his ear—but only hard enough to sting.

He missed her every day.

But apart from those members of his family he had never met anyone immune to his stare. Until now.

From Amalie there was not so much as a flicker, just a shake of her head and her long hair, which was in dire need of a good brush, falling into her eyes. She swiped it away.

Talos sighed, shook his head regretfully and

rubbed his chin, making a great show of disappointment.

Amalie cradled her mug and took a sip of the hot coffee, willing her nerves to stay hidden from his piercing gaze.

All her life she'd had to deal with huge personalities and even huger egos. It had taught her the importance of keeping her emotions tucked away. If the enemy—and at that very moment Talos *was* an enemy to her, she could feel it—detected any weakness then they would pounce. Never make it easy for them. Never give them the advantage.

She had never found it so hard to remain passive. *Never.* Not since she'd been twelve and the nerves she'd fought so hard to contain had taken control of her. The fear and humiliation she'd experienced on that occasion felt as strong today as they had then.

But there was something about this man that *did* things to her; to her mind, to her senses. Inside her belly, a cauldron bubbled.

Talos reached for his briefcase, and for one tiny moment she thought she had won and that he would leave. Except then he placed it on the table and opened it.

'I have tried appealing to your better nature. I

have tried appealing to your greed. I have given you numerous chances to accept the easy way...'

He removed a sheaf of papers and held them up for her to see. 'These are the deeds to the Théâtre de la Musique. You are welcome to read through them. You will see they confirm me as the new owner.'

Stunned into silence, all Amalie could do was shake her head.

'Would you like to read them?'

She continued shaking her head, staring from the documents in his hand to his unsmiling face.

'How is it possible?' she whispered, trying to comprehend what this could mean—for her, for the orchestra...

'I put my offer in on Saturday evening. The purchase was completed an hour ago.'

'But how is this possible?' she repeated. 'This is *France*. The home of bureaucracy and red tape.'

'Money and power talk.'

He placed the deeds back in his briefcase and leaned forward, bringing his face to within inches of hers. Any closer and she'd be able to feel his breath on her face. 'I am a prince. I have money—a lot of it—and I have power. A lot of it. You would be wise to remember that.'

Then he leant back in his chair and drank his coffee, all the while his laser eyes burned into her.

She squeezed her mug, suddenly terrified to lose her grip on it. The implications were forming an orderly queue in her brain.

'Now I am the owner of the theatre I am wondering what I will do with the building and the orchestra it houses. You see, the previous owner was so struck with greed at the amount I offered he made no stipulations for the sale...' He drained the last of his coffee and pushed his mug away so it rested against hers. 'Take the solo, *despinis*, and I will throw so much money at the theatre the crowds will come flocking back and your orchestra will be the toast of Paris. Refuse and I will turn it into a hotel.'

The jostling in her brain stopped. The implications came loud and clear, with clanging bells and ringing sirens.

'You're blackmailing me,' she said starkly. 'You're actually trying to *blackmail* me.'

He shrugged indifferently and pushed his chair back. 'Call it what you will.'

'I call it blackmail. And blackmail is illegal.'

'Tell it to the police.' He displayed his white

teeth. 'However, before you call them I should advise you that I have diplomatic immunity.'

'That is *low*.'

'I can and will go even lower. You see, little songbird, I have the power to ensure you never play the violin professionally again. I can blacken your name, and the names of all those you play with, so that no orchestra—not even a provincial amateur one—would touch you.'

The bubbling cauldron moved from her belly to her head, her brain feeling as if it were boiling with poison. Never had she felt such hate towards another human.

'Get out of my house.'

'Worry not, little songbird, I am ready to leave now.' He looked at his watch. 'I will return in six hours. You can give me your considered answer then.'

Her *considered answer*?

He was threatening to destroy her career, and the careers of her friends and colleagues, and he wanted her *considered answer*?

The cauldron toppled, sending a surge of fire pulsing through her, bringing her to her feet and to his side. Even with him seated and Amalie on her feet the physical imbalance between them was all too apparent. Fear and anger collided in her and she grabbed his arm, as if the force of her will could drag him to his feet and out of her home.

'I said get out of my house!' she shouted, pulling at him, uncaring that holding his arm was akin to holding a steel boulder. 'I don't care if you're a stupid prince *or* about your stupid diplomatic immunity—get *out*!'

With reflexes that would put a cat to shame, Talos yanked her wrists together and pinned the pair of them inside one of his giant hands.

'So you *do* have fire under that pale skin,' he murmured. 'I did wonder.'

'Let go of me right now,' she demanded, panic pulsing through her which only increased when he twisted—pirouetted—her around to sit on his lap, keeping a firm hold on her wrists.

Instinct made her lift her leg and kick back at him. The heel of her bare foot connected with his shin, the pain lancing through her immediate.

For Talos, she might as well have been a toddler doing their worst. He gave absolutely no reaction to her kick other than to wrap his free arm around her waist to secure her to him, ensnaring her even more effectively.

'I feel that hurt you more than it did me,' he said,

holding her trapped hands up to examine them. 'Such elegant fingers... Now, are you going to be a good girl and behave yourself if I let you go?'

'If you call me a good girl again I'll...'

'What? Kick me again?'

She bucked, but it was a futile gesture. It was like being trapped in steel.

Except it wasn't steel. It was solid man. And his fingers were digging not unpleasantly into the side of her waist.

'You're scaring me.' It was part truth. *Something* was scaring her. Terrifying her.

'I know, and I apologise. I will let you go when you assure me that you have your emotions under control and will not lash out at me again.'

Strangely, the deep, rough timbre of his voice had the desired effect, calming her enough to stop her struggling against him.

Clamping her lips together, she forced herself to breathe, and as she did so she inhaled a darkly masculine scent. *His* scent.

She swallowed the moisture that filled her mouth, suddenly aware of his breath, hot in her hair. Every one of her senses was heightened.

She couldn't choke another breath in. Her heart was beating so hard she could hear it echo in her ears. And in the silence that ensued she felt Talos's huge form stiffen too, from the strong thighs she was sat upon to the giant hands holding her in their snare.

She could no longer hear or feel his breath.

The only sound in her ears was the thrumming of her blood.

And then he released her hands and pushed her to her feet.

On legs that trembled, she shot to the other side of the kitchen.

Now she could breathe, but her breaths were ragged, her chest hurting with the exertion.

For his part, Talos calmly shrugged his muscular arms into his trench coat, wrapped his navy scarf around his neck and clasped his briefcase.

'Six hours, *despinis*. I will respect your decision—but know that should your answer continue to be negative the consequences will be real and immediate.'

Amalie's phone vibrated.

She pounced on it. *'Maman?'*

'Chérie, I have found out some things.'

That was typical of her mother—getting straight

to the point. There didn't exist a sliver of silence that her mother's voice couldn't fill.

'I could not reach Pierre directly.'

She sounded put out—as if Pierre Gaskin should have been holding on to his phone on the remote chance that Colette Barthez, the most famous classical singer in the world, deigned to call him.

'But I spoke to his charming assistant, who told me he arrived late to the office this morning, gave every employee five hundred euros and said he was taking the next three months off. He was last seen setting his satnav to take him to Charles de Gaulle,' she added, referring to France's largest airport.

'So it looks as if he *has* sold it, then,' Amalie murmured.

Only two weeks ago Pierre Gaskin—the owner or, as she now firmly believed, the *former* owner of the Théâtre de la Musique—had been struggling to pay the heating bill for the place.

'It looks that way, *chérie*. So tell me,' her mother went on, '*why* has Prince Talos brought the theatre? I didn't know he was a patron of the arts.'

'No idea,' she answered, her skin prickling at the mention of his name. She kneaded her brow, aware that this must be something like her tenth lie of the weekend.

What a mess.

She hadn't told her mother anything of what had happened that weekend—she didn't have the strength to handle *her* reaction on top of everything else—had only asked her to use her contacts to see if there was any truth that the theatre had been sold to Talos Kalliakis.

Now she had the answer.

Talos hadn't been bluffing. But then she hadn't really thought he had been, had turned to her mother only out of a futile sense of having to do *something* rather than any real hope.

'I knew his father, Prince Lelantos...'

Her mother's voice took on a dreamlike quality. It was a sound Amalie recognised, having been her mother's confidante of the heart since the age of twelve.

'I sang for him once. He was such a...' she scrambled for the right word '...*man*!'

'*Maman*, I need to go now.'

'Of course, *chérie*. If you meet Prince Talos again, send him my regards.'

'I will.'

Turning her phone off and placing it on the table, Amalie drew her hands down her face.

There was only one thing left that she could do. She was going to have to tell Talos Kalliakis the truth.

CHAPTER THREE

WHEN TALOS PUNCHED his finger to the bell of Amalie's front door he knew she must have been waiting for him. She pulled the door open before his hand was back by his side.

She stared at him impassively, as if what had occurred between them earlier had never happened. As if she hadn't lost her calm veneer.

Without a word being exchanged, he followed her into the kitchen.

On the table lay a tray of pastries and two plates. A pot of coffee had just finished percolating. Amalie was dressed for her part, having donned a pair of black jeans that hugged her slender frame and a silver scoop-necked top. Her straight dark hair had been brushed back into a loose bun at the nape of her slender neck. She wore no make-up, and the freckles across her nose were vivid in the harsh light beaming from above them.

It was clear to him that she had seen reason. And why on earth would she not? She was a professional musician. He shouldn't have to resort to blackmail.

Time was running out. For the gala. For his grandfather. The chemotherapy he was undergoing had weakened him badly. There were days when he couldn't leave his bed—barely had the strength to retch into a bucket. Other days Talos found him in good spirits, happy to sit outside and enjoy the Agon sunshine in the sprawling palace gardens.

Talos remembered again that he had planned to return home after the auditions on Saturday and spend the rest of the weekend with his grandfather. Instead he'd been compelled to force through— and quickly—the purchase of that awful Parisian building. And for what? Because the only professional violinist he'd found capable of doing justice to his grandmother's final composition was playing hardball.

No one played hardball with Talos Kalliakis. *No one.* To find this slender thing standing up to him...

But she had seen reason. That was all that mattered now.

He allowed himself a smile at his victory, and sat in the chair he'd vacated only six hours before.

Defeat had never crossed his mind. It was regrettable that he'd had to resort to blackmail to get his own way but time was of the essence. The Jubilee was only a month away. There was still time for her to learn the piece to performance standard and for her orchestra to learn the accompanying music. He wanted them note-perfect before they took to the palace stage.

Amalie's arm brushed against his as she placed a mug in front of him. He found his attention caught by her fingers, as it had been earlier, when he'd had them trapped in his hand. It was the nails at the end of those long, elegant fingers that had really struck him. The nails of her left hand were short and blunt. The nails of her right hand were much longer and shapely. He'd puzzled over those nails all day…over what they reminded him of.

He'd also puzzled over the reaction that had swept through him when he'd pinned her to his lap after her anger had rushed to the surface.

Talos was a man who enjoyed the company of beautiful women. And beautiful women liked *him*. Women he didn't know would catch his eye and hold it for a beat too long. When they learned who he was their gazes would stay fixed, suggestion and invitation ringing from them.

Never had he met a woman who so obviously

disliked him. Never had he met anyone—man or woman—outside his immediate family who would deny him anything he wanted.

Amalie Cartwright was a pretty woman in her own unique way. The defiant attitude she'd displayed towards him infuriated and intrigued him in equal measure.

What, he wondered, would it be like to light the fire he'd glimpsed that morning in a more intimate setting?

What would it take to twist that fire and anger into passion?

He had felt the shift in her when her whole body had stilled and her breath had shortened and then stopped. The same time his own breath had stopped. One moment he'd been staring at her fingers with bemusement, the next his body had been filled with an awareness so strong it had knocked the air out of him.

He'd never experienced a reaction like it.

And now, watching her take the same seat as she had that morning, he could feel that awareness stirring within him again.

The following month held infinite possibilities...

'Monsieur,' she said once she had settled herself

down and placed her green gaze on him, 'earlier you appealed to my better nature—'

'Which you disregarded,' he interjected.

She bowed her head in acknowledgement. 'I had my reasons, which I am going to share with you in the hope of appealing to *your* better nature.'

He regarded her carefully but kept silent, waiting for her to speak her mind. Surely she wasn't trying another angle to turn the solo down?

'I'm sorry but I lied to you—I do not have a prior engagement on the gala weekend.' She gnawed on her bottom lip before continuing. 'I suffer from stage fright.'

The idea was so ludicrous Talos shook his head in disbelief and laughed.

'You?' he said, not bothering to hide his incredulity. 'You—the daughter of Colette Barthez and Julian Cartwright—suffer from *stage fright*?'

'You know who I am?'

'I know exactly who you are.' He folded his arms, his brief, incredulous mirth evaporating. 'I made it my business to know.'

He caught a flash of truculence in those green eyes, the first sign that the calm façade she wore was nothing but a front.

'Your French mother is the most successful

mezzo-soprano in the world. I admit I hadn't heard of your father before today, but I understand he is a famous English violinist. I also learned that your father once played at Carnegie Hall with my grandmother, when he was first establishing himself.'

He leaned forward to rest his chin on his hands.

'*You* were a noted child prodigy until the age of twelve, when your parents removed you from the spotlight so you could concentrate on your education. You became a professional musician at the age of twenty, when you joined the ranks of the Orchestre National de Paris as a second violin—a position you still hold five years on.'

She shrugged, but her face remained taut. 'What you have described is something any person with access to the internet could find out in thirty seconds. My parents didn't remove me from the spotlight because of my education—that is what my mother told the press, because she couldn't bear the shame of having a daughter unable to perform in public.'

'If you are "unable to perform in public", how do you explain the fact that you *perform in public* at least once a week with your orchestra?'

'I'm a second violin. I sit at the back of the orchestra. We have an average of eighty musicians playing at any given performance. The audience's eyes are not on me but on the collective orchestra. It's two different things. If I play at your grandfather's gala everyone's eyes will be on *me* and I will freeze. It will bring humiliation to me, to my mother—and to your grandfather. Is that what you want? To have the world's eyes witness your star performer frozen on stage, unable to play a note?'

The only person who wouldn't be ashamed of her was her father. She might have referred to it as a joint decision by her parents, but in truth it had been her father who'd gone against her mother's wishes and pulled her out of the spotlight. He'd been the one to assure her that it was okay to play just for the love of the music, even if it was only in the privacy of her own bedroom.

Talos's eyes narrowed, a shrewd expression emanating from them. 'How do I know you aren't lying to me right now?'

'I...'

'By your own admission you lied about being busy on the gala weekend.'

'It was a lie of necessity.'

'No lie is necessary. If you can't handle eyes on you when you play, how were you able to join the orchestra in the first place?'

'It was a blind audition. Everyone who applied had to play behind a screen so there could be no bias. And, before you ask, of course I practise and rehearse amongst my colleagues, But that is a world away from standing up on a stage and feeling hundreds of eyes staring at you.'

He shook his head slowly, his light brown eyes unreadable. 'I am in two minds here. Either you are speaking the truth or you are telling another lie.'

'I am speaking the truth. You need to find another soloist.'

'I think not. Nerves and stage fright are things that can be overcome, but finding another soloist who can do justice to my grandmother's final composition is a different matter.'

Never mind that time had almost run out. He could spend the rest of his life searching and not find anyone whose playing touched him the way Amalie's had in those few minutes he had listened to her.

Talos had never settled for second best in his life and he wasn't about to start now.

'What do you know about my island?' he asked her.

She looked confused at the change of direction. 'Not much. It's near Crete, isn't it?'

'Crete is our nearest neighbour. Like the Cretans, we are descended from the Minoans. Throughout the centuries Agon has been attacked by the Romans, the Ottomans and the Venetians—to name a few. We repelled them all. Only the Venetians managed to occupy us, and just for a short period. My people, under the leadership of the warrior Ares Patakis, of whom I am a direct descendent, rose against the occupiers and expelled them from our land. No other nation has occupied our shores since. History tells our story. Agonites will not be oppressed or repressed. We will fight until our last breath for our freedom.'

He paused to take a sip of his coffee. He had to hand it to her: she had excellent taste.

'You are probably wondering why I am telling you all this,' he said.

'I *am* trying to understand the relevance,' she admitted thoughtfully.

'It is to give you an awareness of the stock that I, my family and our people come from. We are fighters. There isn't an Agonite alive who would back down in the face of adversity. Stage fright? Nerves? Those are issues to be fought and conquered. And with my help you *will* conquer them.'

Amalie could imagine it only too well. Talos

Kalliakis ready for battle, stripped to nothing but iron battle gear, spear in hand. He would be at the front of any fight.

It was her bad fortune that he had chosen to fight *her*.

But her stage fright *wasn't* a fight. It was just a part of her, something she had long ago accepted.

Her life was nice and cosy. Simple. No drama, no histrionics. She refused to allow the tempestuousness of her childhood seep its way into her adult life.

'I have arranged with your directors for you to come to Agon in a couple of days and to stay until the gala. Your orchestra will start rehearsals immediately and fly out a week before the gala so you can rehearse with them.'

Her pledge to be amiable evaporated. 'Excuse me, but you've done what?'

'It will give you a month in Agon to acclimatise...'

'I don't need to acclimatise. Agon is hardly the middle of a desert.'

'It will also give you a month to prepare yourself perfectly for the solo,' he continued, ignoring her interruption, although his eyes flashed another warning at her. 'No distractions.'

'But…'

'Your stage fright is something that *will* be over-come,' he said, with all the assurance of a man who had never been struck with anything as weak as nerves. 'I will see to it personally.'

He stopped speaking, leaving a pause she knew she was supposed to fill, but all she could think was how badly she wanted to throw something at him, to curse this hateful man who was attempting to destroy the comfortable, quiet life she had made for herself away from the spotlight.

'Despinis?'

She looked up to find those laser eyes striking through her again, as if he could reach right in and see what she was thinking.

'Do you accept the solo?' His voice hardened to granite. 'Or do I have to make one hundred musicians redundant? Do I have to destroy one hundred careers, including your own? Have no doubt—I will do it. I will destroy you all.'

She closed her eyes and breathed deeply, trying to extinguish the panic clawing at her throat.

She believed him. This was no idle threat. He *could* destroy her career. She had no idea how he would do it, she knew only that he could.

If she didn't loathe him so much she would wonder why he was prepared to take such dark measures to get her agreement. As it was, she couldn't give a flying viola as to his reasons.

If she didn't comply he would take away the only thing she could do.

But how could she agree to do it? The last time she'd performed solo she'd been surrounded by her parents' arty friends—musicians, actors, writers, singers. She'd humiliated herself and her mother in front of every one of them. How could she stand on a stage with dignitaries and heads of state watching her and not be shredded by the same nerves? That was if she even made it on to the stage.

The one time she'd tried after the awful incident had left her hospitalised. And what she remembered most clearly about that dreadful time was her father's fury at her mother for forcing her. He'd accused her of selfishness and of using their only child as a toy.

A lump formed in Amalie's throat as she recalled them separating mere weeks later, her father gaining primary custody of her.

She was lucky, though. If times got really hard she knew she could rely on both her parents to bail her out. She would never go hungry. She would never lose her home. Her colleagues weren't all so fortunate. Not many of them were blessed with wealthy parents.

She thought of kindly Juliette, who was seven months pregnant with her third child. Of Louis, who only last week had booked a bank-breaking holiday with his family to Australia. Grumbling Giles, who moaned every month when his mortgage payment was taken from his account…

All those musicians, all those office workers…

All unaware that their jobs, security and reputations hung in the balance.

She stared at Talos, willing him to feel every ounce of her hate.

'Yes, I'll come. But the consequences are something *you* will have to live with.'

Amalie gazed out of the window and got her first glimpse of Agon. As the plane made its descent she stared transfixed as golden beaches emerged alongside swathes of green, high mountains and built-up areas of pristine white buildings… And then they touched down, bouncing along the runway before coming to a final smooth stop.

Keeping a firm grip on her violin, she followed her fellow business-class passengers out and down the metal stairs. After the slushy iciness of Paris in March, the temperate heat was a welcome delight.

From the economy section bounded excited children and frazzled parents, there to take advantage of the sunshine Agon was blessed with, where spring and summer came earlier than to its nearest neighbour, Crete. She hadn't considered that she would be going to an island famed as a holiday destination for families and historical buffs alike. In her head she'd thought of Agon as a prison—as dark and dangerous as the man who had summoned her there.

Amalie had travelled to over thirty countries in her life, but never had she been in an airport as fresh and welcoming as the one in Agon. Going through Arrivals was quick; her luggage arriving on the conveyor belt even quicker.

A man waited in the exit lounge, holding up her name on a specially laminated board. Polite introductions out of the way, he took the trolley holding her luggage from her and led the way out to a long, black car parked in what was clearly the prime space of the whole car park.

Everything was proceeding exactly as had been stated in the clipped email Talos's private secretary had sent to her the day before. It had contained a detailed itinerary, from the time a car would be collecting her from her house all the way through to her estimated time of arrival at the villa that would be her home for the next month.

As the chauffeur navigated the roads she was able to take further stock of the island. Other than expecting it to be as dangerous as the youngest of its princes, she'd had no preconceptions. She was glad. Talos Kalliakis might be a demon sent to her from Hades, but his island was stunning.

Mementoes of Agon's early Greek heritage were everywhere, from the architecture to the road signs in the same common language. But Agon was now a sovereign island, autonomous in its rule. The thing that struck her most starkly was how clean everything was, from the well-maintained roads to the buildings and homes they drove past. When they went past a harbour she craned her neck to look more closely at the rows of white yachts stationed there—some of them as large as cruise liners.

Soon they were away from the town and winding higher into the hills and mountains. Her mouth dropped open when she caught her first glimpse of the palace, standing proudly on a hill much in the same way as the ancient Greeks had built their most sacred monuments. Enormous and sprawling, it had a Middle Eastern flavour to it, as if it had been built for a great sultan centuries ago.

But it wasn't to the palace that she was headed. No sooner had it left her sight than the chauffeur slowed down, pausing while a wrought-iron gate inched open, then drove up to a villa so large it could have been a hotel. Up the drive he took them, and then round to the back of the villa's grounds, travelling for another mile until he came to a much smaller dwelling at the edge of the extensive villa's garden—a generously sized white stone cottage.

An elderly man, with a shock of white hair flapping in the breeze above a large bald spot, came out of the front door to greet them.

'Good evening, *despinis*,' he said warmly. 'I am Kostas.'

Explaining that he ran the main villa for His Highness Prince Talos, he showed her around the cottage that would be her home for the month. The small kitchen was well stocked and a daily delivery of fresh fruit, breads and dairy products would be brought to her. If she wished to eat her meals in the main villa she only had to pick up the phone and let them know; likewise if she wished to have meals delivered to the cottage.

'The villa has a gym, a swimming pool, and spa facilities you are welcome to use whenever you wish,' he said before he left. 'There are also a number of cars you can use if you wish to travel anywhere, or we can arrange for a driver to take you.'

So Talos didn't intend to keep her prisoner in the cottage? That was handy to know.

She'd envisaged him collecting her from the airport, locking her in a cold dungeon and refusing to let her out until she was note-perfect with his grandmother's composition and all her demons had been banished.

Thinking about it sent a tremor racing up her spine.

She wondered what great psychiatrist Talos would employ to 'fix' her. She would laugh if the whole thing didn't terrify her so much. Whoever he employed had better get a move on. She had exactly four weeks and two days until she had to stand on the stage for the King of Agon's Jubilee Gala. In those thirty days she had to learn an entirely new composition, her orchestra had to learn the accompanying score, and she had to overcome the nerves that had paralysed her for over half her lifetime.

CHAPTER FOUR

THE MORNING CAME, crisp and blue. After a quick shower Amalie donned her favourite black jeans and a plum shirt, then made herself a simple breakfast, which she took out to eat on her private veranda. As she ate yogurt and honey, and sipped at strong coffee—she'd been delighted to find a brand-new state-of-the-art coffee machine, with enough pods to last her a year—she relaxed into a wicker chair and let the cool breeze brush over her. After all the bustle of Paris it felt wonderful to simply *be*.

If she closed off her mind she could forget why she was there...pretend she was on some kind of holiday.

Her tranquillity didn't last long.

After going back inside to try another of the coffee-machine pods—this time opting for the mocha—she came back onto the veranda to find Talos sitting on her vacated chair, helping himself to the cubes of melon she'd cut up.

'Good morning, little songbird,' he said with a flash of straight white teeth.

Today he was dressed casually, in baggy khaki canvas trousers, black boots and a long-sleeved V-necked grey top. He was unshaven and his hair looked as if it had been tamed with little more than the palm of a hand. As she leaned over the table to place her mug down she caught his freshly showered scent.

'Is that for me?' he asked, nodding at the mug in her shaking hand.

She shrugged, affecting nonchalance at his unexpected appearance. 'If you don't mind sharing my germs.'

'I'm sure a beautiful woman like you doesn't have anything so nasty as germs.'

She raised a suspicious eyebrow, shivering as his deep bass voice reverberated through her skin, before turning back into the cottage, glad of an excuse to escape for a moment and gather herself. Placing a new pod in the machine, she willed her racing heart to still.

He'd startled her with his presence, that was all. She'd received an email from his private secretary the evening before, while eating the light evening meal she'd prepared for herself, stating that the score would be brought to her at the cottage mid-morning. There had been nothing mentioned about the Prince himself bothering to join her. Indeed, once she'd realised she wasn't staying in the palace she'd hoped not to see him again.

When she went back outside he was cradling the mug, an expression of distaste wrinkling his face. 'What *is* this?'

'Mocha.'

'It is disgusting.'

'Don't drink it, then.'

'I won't.' He placed it on the table and gave it a shove with his fingers to move it away from him. He nodded at her fresh cup. 'What's that one?'

'Mocha—to replace the one you kidnapped. If you want something different, the coffee machine's in the kitchen.' The contract she'd signed had said nothing about making coffee for him.

That evil contract...

She dragged her thoughts away before her brain could rage anew. If she allowed herself to fume over the unfairness, her wits would be dulled, and she already knew to her bitter cost that she needed her wits about her when dealing with this man.

As she sat herself in the vacant chair, unsubtly moving it away from his side, Talos reached for an apple from the plate of fruit she'd brought out with her. Removing a stumpy metal object from his trouser pocket, he pressed a button on the side and a blade at least five inches long unfolded. The snap it made jolted her.

Talos noticed her flinch. 'Does my knife bother you?'

'Not at all. Did you get that little thing when you were a Boy Scout?'

Her dismissive tone grated on him more than it should have. *She* grated on him more than she should.

'This little thing?' He swivelled the chair, narrowed his eyes and flicked his wrist. The knife sliced through the air, landing point-first in the cherry tree standing a good ten feet from them, embedding itself in the trunk.

He didn't bother hiding his satisfaction. 'That *little thing* was a present from my grandfather when I graduated from Sandhurst.'

'I'm impressed,' she said flatly. 'I always thought Sandhurst was for gentlemen.'

Was that yet *another* insult?

'Was there a reason you came to see me other than to massacre a defenceless tree?' she asked.

He got to his feet. 'I've brought the score to you.'

He strode to the cherry tree, gripped the handle of the knife and pulled it out. This knife was a badge of honour—the mark of becoming a man, a replacement for the Swiss Army penknife each Kalliakis prince had been given on his tenth birthday. There was an apple tree in the palace gardens whose trunk still bore the scars of the three young Princes' attempts at target practice two decades before.

Back at the table, aware of wary sapphire eyes watching his every movement, he wiped the blade on his trousers, then picked up his selected apple and proceeded to peel it, as had been his intention when he'd first removed the knife from his pocket. The trick was to peel it in one single movement before the white of the inside started to brown—a relic from his childhood, when his father would peel an apple before slicing it and eating the chunks, and something he in turn had learned from *his* father. Of course Talos's father hadn't lived long enough to see any of his sons master it.

Carrying a knife was a habit all the Kalliakis men shared. Talos had no idea what had compelled him to throw it at the tree.

Had he been trying to get a rise out of her?

Never had he been in the company of anyone, let alone a woman, to whom his presence was so clearly unwelcome. People wanted his company. They sought it, they yearned to keep it. No one treated him with indifference.

And yet this woman did.

Other than that spark of fire in her home, when he'd played his trump card, she'd remained cool and poised in all their dealings, her body language giving nothing away. Only now, as he pushed the large binder that contained the solo towards her, did she show any emotion, her eyes flickering, her breath sharpening.

'Is this it?' she asked, opening the binder to peer at what lay inside.

'You look as if you're afraid to touch it.'

'I've never held anything made by a royal hand.'

He studied her, curiosity driving through him. 'You look respectfully towards a sheet of music, yet show no respect towards me, a prince of this land.'

'Respect is earned, *monsieur*, and you have done nothing to earn mine.'

Why wasn't she scared of him?

'On this island our people respect the royal family. It comes as automatically as breathing.'

'Did you use brute force to gain it? Or do you prefer simple blackmail?'

'Five hundred years ago it was considered treason to show insolence towards a member of the Agon royal family.'

'If that law were still in force now I bet your subjects' numbers would be zero.'

'The law was brought in by the senate, out of gratitude to my family for keeping this island safe from our enemies. My ancestors were the ones to abolish it.'

'I bet your subjects partied long into the night when it was abolished.'

'Do not underestimate the people of this island, *despinis*,' he said, his ire rising at her flippant attitude. 'Agonites are not and never will be subjects. This is not a dictatorship. The Kalliakis family members remain the island's figureheads by overwhelming popular consent. Our blood is their blood—their blood is our blood. They will celebrate my grandfather's Jubilee Gala with as much enthusiasm as if they were attending a party for their own grandfather.'

Her pale cheeks were tinged with a light pinkness. She swallowed. 'I didn't mean to insult your family, *monsieur*.'

He bowed his head in acceptance of her apology.

'Only you.'

'Only me?'

Her sapphire eyes sparked, but there was no light in them. 'I only meant to insult *you*.'

'If the palace dungeons hadn't been turned into a tourist attraction I would have you thrown into them.'

'And it's comments like that which make me happy to insult you. You blackmail me into coming here, you threaten my career and the careers of my friends, and you make me sign a contract including a penalty for my not performing at your grandfather's gala: the immediate disbandment of the Orchestre National de Paris... So, yes, I will happily take any opportunity I can to insult you.'

He stretched out his long legs and ran his fingers through his hair. 'It's comments like that which make me wonder...'

Her face scrunched up in a question.

'You see, little songbird, I wonder how a woman who professes to have stage fright so bad she cannot stand on a stage and play the instrument she was born to play has the nerve to show such disrespect to me. Do I not frighten you?'

She paused a beat before answering. 'You are certainly imposing.'

'That is not an answer.'

'The only thing that frightens me is the thought of standing on the stage for your grandfather's gala.' A lie, she knew, but Amalie would sooner stand on the stage naked than admit that she was *terrified* of him. Or terrified of something about him. The darkness. *His* darkness.

'Then I suggest you start learning the music for it.' He rose to his feet, his dark features set in an impenetrable mask. 'I will collect you at seven this evening and you can fill me in on your feelings for it.'

'Collect me for what?'

'Your first session in overcoming your stage fright.'

'Right.'

She bit her lip. Strangely, she'd envisaged Talos bringing an army of shrinks to *her*. That was what her mother had done during Amalie's scheduled visits after her parents' divorce. Anything would have been better than Colette Barthez's daughter being photographed at the door of a psychiatrist's office. The press wouldn't have been able to do anything with the pictures, or print any story about it, her mother had seen to that, but secrets had a way of not remaining secret once more people knew about them.

'Wear something sporty.'

'Sporty?' she asked blankly.

'I'm taking you to my gym.'

She rubbed at an eyebrow. 'I'm confused. Why would we see a shrink at your gym?'

'I never said anything about a shrink.'

'You did.'

'No, little songbird, I said *I* would help you overcome your stage fright.'

'I didn't think you meant it literally.' For the first time in her life she understood what *aghast* meant. *She* was aghast. 'You don't really mean that *you're* planning to fix me?'

He gazed down at her, unsmiling. 'Have you undertaken professional help before?'

'My mother wheeled out every psychiatrist she could get in France and England.'

'And none of them were able to help you.' It was a statement, not a question. 'You have a huge amount of spirit in your blood. It is a matter of harnessing it to your advantage. I will teach you to fight through your nerves and conquer them.'

'But…'

'Seven o'clock. Be ready.'

He strode away, his huge form relaxed. Too relaxed. So relaxed it infuriated her even more, turning her fear and anger up to a boil. Without thinking, she reached for a piece of discarded apple core and threw it at him. Unbelievably, it hit the back of his neck.

He turned around slowly, then crouched down to pick up the offending weapon, which he looked at briefly before fixing his eyes on her. Even with the distance between them the darkness in those eyes was unmistakable. As was the danger.

Amalie gulped in air, her lungs closing around it and refusing to let go.

Do I not frighten you...?

Frightened didn't even begin to describe the terror racing through her blood at that moment—a terror that increased with each long step he took back towards her.

Fighting with everything she possessed to keep herself collected, she refused to turn away from his black gaze.

It wasn't until he loomed over her, his stare piercing right through her, that she felt rather than saw the swirl flickering in it.

'You should be careful, little songbird. A lesser

man than me might take the throwing of an apple core as some kind of mating ritual.'

His deep, rough voice was pitched low with an underlying playfulness that scared her almost more than anything else.

The thing that terrified her the most was the beating of her heart, so loud she was certain he must be able to hear it. Not the staccato beat of terror but the raging thrum of awareness.

He was so close she could see the individual stalks of stubble across his strong jawline, the flare of his nostrils, and the silver hue of the scar lancing his eyebrow. Her hand rose, as if a magnet had burrowed under her skin and was being drawn to reach up and touch his face...

Before she'd raised it more than a couple of inches, Talos leaned closer and whispered directly into her ear. 'I think I *do* frighten you. But not in the same way I frighten others.'

With that enigmatic comment he straightened, stepped away from her, nodded a goodbye, and then headed back to his villa.

Only when he was a good fifteen paces away did her lungs relax enough to expel the stale air, and the remnants of his woody, musky smell took its place, hitting her right in the sinuses, then spreading through her as if her body was consuming it.

If Amalie's long-sleeved white top that covered her bottom and her dark blue leggings strayed too far from the 'sporty' brief he'd given her, Talos made no mention of it when she opened her door to him at precisely seven that evening. He did, however, stare at the flat canvas shoes on her feet.

'Do you not have any proper trainers?'

'No.'

He gave a sound like a grunt.

'I'm not really into exercise,' she admitted.

'You are for the next thirty days.'

'I find it boring.'

'That's because you're not doing it right.'

It was like arguing with a plank. Except a plank would be more responsive to her argument.

But a plank wouldn't evoke such an immediate reaction within her. Or prevent her lungs from working properly.

For his part, Talos was dressed in dark grey sports pants that fitted his long, muscular legs perfectly, and a black T-shirt that stretched across his chest, showcasing his broad warrior-like athleticism.

The stubble she remembered from the morning was even thicker now…

It was like gazing at a pure shot of testosterone. The femininity right in her core responded to it, a slow ache burning in her belly, her heart racing to a thrum with one look.

He walked her to his car; a black Maserati that even in the dusk of early evening gleamed. She stepped into the passenger side, the scent of leather filling her senses.

She'd never known anyone fill the interior of a car the way Talos did. Beside him she felt strangely fragile, as if she were made of porcelain rather than flesh and blood.

She blinked the strange thought away and knotted her fingers together, silently praying the journey would be short.

'How did you find the composition?' he asked after a few minutes of silence.

'Beautiful.'

It was the only word she could summon. For five hours she had worked her way through the piece, bar by bar, section by section. She was a long way from mastering it, or understanding all its intricacies, but already the underlying melody had made itself known and had her hooked.

'You are certain you will be ready to perform it in a month's time?'

Opportunity suddenly presented itself to her gift-wrapped. 'A composition of this complexity could take me *months* to master. You would do far better to employ a soloist who can get a quicker handle on it.'

He was silent for a moment, and when he spoke there was an amused tinge to his voice. 'You don't give up, do you?'

'I don't know what you mean.'

'Oh, I think you do. I remind you, *despinis*, that you signed a contract.'

'And *you* said you would get me help.'

'I said I would help you and that is what I am doing.'

He brought the car to a stop at the front of a large cream building and faced her. Even in the dark she could see the menace on his features.

'I will accept no excuses. You *will* learn the composition and you *will* play it at the gala and you *will* do it justice. If you fail in any of those conditions then I will impose the contracted penalty.'

He didn't have to elaborate any further. The 'contracted penalty' meant turning the theatre into a hotel and causing the disbandment of the orchestra.

That penalty loomed large in her mind: the threat to ruin every member of the orchestra's reputation...her own most especially.

'Understand, though,' he continued, 'that I am a man of my word. I said I would ensure that you are mentally fit to get on the stage and play, and that is what I will do. Starting now.'

He got out of the car and opened the boot, pulling out a black sports bag. 'Follow me.'

Not having any choice, she followed him into the building.

The first thing that hit her was the smell.

She'd never been in a men's locker room before, but this was *exactly* what she'd imagined it would smell like: sweat and testosterone.

The second thing to hit her was the noise.

The third thing was the sight of a man with a flat nose, standing behind the reception desk at the entrance, spotting Talos and getting straight to his feet, a huge grin spreading over his face.

The two men greeted each other with bumped fists and a babble of Greek that ended with Talos giving the man a hearty slap on the back before indicating to Amalie to follow him. As they walked away she couldn't help but notice the blatant adoration on the flat-nosed man's face. Not a romantic adoration—she'd witnessed *that* enough times from her mother to know what it looked like—but more a look of reverence.

Past the reception area, they slipped through a door and entered the most enormous room.

Silently she took it all in: the square ring in the corner, the huge blue mats laid out in a square in another, the punching bags dangling at seemingly random places...

'Is this a *boxing* gym?'

He raised a hefty shoulder. 'I've boxed since my childhood.'

'I can't *box!*'

He gazed down at her hands. 'No. You can't. Throwing a punch at even the softest target has the danger of breaking a finger.'

She hadn't thought of that—had been too busy thinking that she'd never hit anyone or anything in her life and had always considered boxing to be the most barbaric of sports. It was fitting to learn that it was Talos's sport of choice. Her encounters with him were the closest she'd ever come to actually hitting someone.

He pointed to the corner with the blue mats. A tall, athletic blonde woman was chatting to a handful of men and women, all decked out in proper sports gear. 'That is Melina, one of the instructors here. I've signed you up for her kickboxing workout.'

Amalie sighed. 'How is enduring a kickboxing workout supposed to make me mentally fit for the stage?'

Without warning he placed his hands on her shoulders and twisted her around, so her back was to him. His thumbs pressed into the spot between her shoulder blades.

'You are rife with tension,' he said.

'Of course I am. I'm here under duress.'

She tried to duck out from his hold but his grip was too strong. *He* was too strong. His thumbs felt huge as they pressed up the nape of her neck. And warm. And surprisingly gentle, despite the strength behind them.

'The workout will help relieve tension and fire up your endorphins.' He laughed—a deep rumble that vibrated through her pores—and released his hold on her. 'All you will do is kick and punch into the air. If it helps, you can pretend I'm standing in front of you, receiving it all.'

She turned back to face him. 'That *will* help.'

The glimmer of humour left him. 'Your aggression needs an outlet.'

'I'm not aggressive!' At least she never had been before. Talos brought something out in her that, while not violent in the sense she'd always associated aggression with, made her feel as if a ferocity had been awoken within her, one that only reared up when she was with him. Or thinking about him. Or dreaming about him…

This workout might just prove to be a blessing after all.

'Maybe not, but the tension you have within you comes from somewhere…'

'That'll be from being here with you,' she grumbled.

'And once you have learned to expel it your mind will be calmer.'

'What about my body? I haven't exercised in for ever.'

His eyes swept up and down her body, taking in every part of her. It felt like a critical assessment of her physique and she squirmed under it. She waited for his verbal assessment but it never came.

'I will introduce you to Melina,' he said, striding away to the growing crowd around the instructor.

Melina's eyes gleamed when she spotted Talos, then narrowed slightly when she caught sight of Amalie, hanging back a little behind him.

Introductions were made and then Talos left them to it, heading to the ring in the corner, where a sparring bout had just started between two teen-age boys. After a quick conversation with their trainer, Simeon, he left the main hall and went into the adjoining gym to start his own workout. He might spar later with Simeon, but first he wanted to warm his body up and get his muscles moving.

It felt as if it had been an age since he'd worked out, although it had only been one day.

Moving through the equipment, following the routine that had served him well since his army days, he found his concentration levels weren't as sharp as usual. Through the glass wall dividing the gym from the main hall he could see the kick-boxing workout underway, and noted how Amalie had placed herself at the back of the pack, how self-conscious her movements were.

He didn't usually enjoy using the treadmill, but today he stayed on it for longer than normal, watching her. The warm-up was over and the session had begun in earnest. As the session progressed her movements went from tentative to a little less so. He could see the concentration on her face as she tried to copy what everyone around her was doing—the way she pivoted on the heel of her left foot before throwing an imaginary hook, the way she put her fists by her face, shifted her weight to her right foot, then brought her left knee up to her chest before kicking out.

She had an excellent centre of gravity, he noted. And for someone who professed to never exercise, her body was delectable, the leggings and long T-shirt she wore showing off her slender form to perfection.

She must have sensed his eyes upon her, for suddenly her gaze was on him, a scowl forming on her pretty face.

He didn't normally find a woman's anger cute, but with Amalie it was like being glared at by a harmless kitten.

Harmless kitten or not, the jabs and kicks she gave from that moment on brought to mind the image of a wildcat. She cut through the air with one particularly vicious right hook and he knew with deep certainty that it was *his* face she'd imagined her fist connecting with.

He reached for his towel and wiped his brow, inhaling deeply, trying to control the burn seeping through him. Watching Amalie work out had a strange hypnotic quality to it—as if she had magical powers pulling his attention to her.

It was time to take his attention elsewhere.

He was at the punching bags when her workout finished. He kept his focus on the bag before him, aware of her approach.

He would have been aware of her even if she hadn't cleared her throat to announce her presence by his side. Tendrils of sensation prickled his skin, and when he turned his attention from the punching bag to her, saw the dampness of her hair and the heightened colour of her cheeks, all he could think about was how she would look under the flames of passion.

'What did you think?' he asked.

Something resembling a smile spread across her face. 'Once I focused and imagined all my punches connecting with your face and all my kicks hitting your abdomen, it was great.'

He laughed. 'And how do you feel now?'

She considered the question, her lips pouting. 'I feel…*good*.'

'Is this the point where I say I told you so?'

She rolled her eyes. 'Are we going to be here much longer? Only I could really do with a shower. And something to eat.'

An image flashed into his mind of her standing naked under hot running water.

'There are showers here, with everything you need.'

'But then I'll have to change back into these sweaty things.'

'We have a selection of gym wear on sale too—I *did* say you would need suitable clothes to work out in. Choose some—and get yourself a decent pair of training shoes.'

'I haven't got any money on me.'

'Not a problem.' He looked over her head and beckoned someone.

A slight young girl of no more than sixteen appeared. Talos said something to her, then addressed Amalie again. 'This is Tessa. She will take you to our clothes store and then show you where the ladies' showers are. I'll meet you upstairs in the café when you're done.'

As soon as they'd headed off he focused back on the punching bag, trying to put aside the images of her naked that insisted on staying at the forefront of his mind.

He threw a particularly hard upper cut at the bag.

This was a singularly unique position he'd put himself in.

Amalie was incredibly desirable. He couldn't pinpoint what exactly it was, but it was as if she had some kind of aura that seeped into his skin and set a charge off inside him. Everything felt so much more heightened. He felt an awareness not only of *her* but also the chemical components that were making *him* feel off the scale. Put simply: being with her made him feel as sexy as hell.

Under any other circumstances he wouldn't hesitate to seduce her. Just imagining those long limbs wrapped around him put him on the path to arousal.

Her awareness of him was strong too—as starkly obvious as her loathing. Lust and loathing… An explosive combination.

But these were not normal circumstances. He had to get her mentally prepared to take on the biggest solo of her life. It was the whole reason she was there. Something told him she wasn't the type of woman to go for the casual affairs he insisted on. Throwing sex into the mix could be like throwing a match into a situation that was already combustible.

He threw one last punch, then took a seat on the bench and, breathing heavily, undid the wraps around his hands, which he always put on even if only sparring with the punching bag. Experience had taught him how brittle the bones in the human hand were. The pain of breakage was negligible, but unless the hand was rested enough to allow the bones to heal it wouldn't set properly, and the boxer would be unable to punch at full power.

Resting a broken hand was as frustrating as desiring a beautiful woman, knowing she desired you too, but knowing you couldn't ever act on it.

CHAPTER FIVE

DESPITE THE LATENESS of the evening, the café upstairs was busy. Amalie had found a small table against the wall, where she could wait for Talos. Aware of the curious glances being thrown her way she pretended to examine the menu.

Testosterone abounded in the café. The vast majority of the patrons were male, all of them muscular, a fair few displaying broken noses and scarred faces. But their muscular physiques were dwarfed when Talos entered the room.

He spotted her immediately, and as he made his way over people stopped him to shake hands or bump fists.

She was glad his attention was taken, if only for a few moments. She pressed a hand to her chest and inhaled as much air into her tight lungs as she could get. The green sports pants and matching T-shirt she'd taken from the gym's sports clothing outlet suddenly felt very close against her skin. Constricting.

He'd changed into a pair of tight-fitting black jeans and a navy blue T-shirt, and had his sports bag slung over his shoulder.

He was a mountain man, and whatever he wore only emphasised his muscularity. Whether he was in a business suit, workout gear or something casual, she couldn't shake the feeling that he would be equally at home with nothing but a loin cloth wrapped around his waist.

'I thought subjects were supposed to kneel before royalty,' she said when he finally joined her.

A smirk appeared on his lips. 'If you want to get on your knees before me, I won't complain.'

She glared at him.

He settled his huge frame onto the chair opposite her. 'You have to admit your comment was an open invitation.'

'Only to someone with a dirty mind…' she said, but her voice trailed into a mumble as the imagery his comment provoked, startling and vivid, sent a pulse searing through her blood strong enough to make her entire face burn.

The fresh scent of his shower gel and the woody musk of his aftershave played under her nose, filling her senses. He still hadn't shaved, his stubble thick and covering his jawline in its entirety.

Certain she'd handed him another gold-plated open invitation, she cast her eyes down before he had a chance to read what was in them.

Instead of the expected quip, he asked in an amused tone, 'What would you like to order?'

As he spoke, he folded his arms onto the table, his biceps bulging with the motion. She should have stayed looking at his face.

Since when did blatant machismo testosterone do it for her?

The male musicians she worked with—especially her fellow violinists—were, on the whole, sensitive creatures physically *and* emotionally. There were always exceptions to the rule, such as Philippe, one of the Orchestre National de Paris's trombone players. Philippe was blond, buff and handsome, and he flirted openly with any woman who caught his eye. He was rumoured to have bedded half the female musicians in the orchestra.

But not Amalie, who found his overt masculinity a complete turn-off. The few boyfriends *she'd* had had been slight, unthreatening men, with gentle natures and a deep appreciation of music. Their evenings together had been spent discussing all things to do with music and the arts in general, with the bedroom not even an afterthought.

So why did Talos, whose physique and masculinity were ten times as potent as anything Philippe could even dream of having, make her feel all hot and squidgy just to look at him? None of her boyfriends had made her feel like he did—as if she wanted nothing more than to rip his clothes off.

'I don't read Greek,' she answered, dragging her vocal cords into working order. 'I wouldn't know what to choose.'

'We don't serve traditional Greek fare here,' he said. 'It's mostly high-carb and high-protein foods like pasta and steak.'

'Do they have burgers?'

He grinned.

'What's so funny?'

'After a hard workout I go for a burger every time.'

'With cheese?'

'It's not right without the cheese.'

'And chips?'

'It wouldn't be a complete meal without them.'

'Cheeseburger and chips for me, then, please.'

'Drink?'

'Coke?'

His sensuous lips widened into a full-blown grin that was as sinful as the food she wanted.

'Two cheeseburgers and chips, and two Cokes coming up.'

He got up from his seat, walked to the counter, fist-bumped the teenage boy working there and gave their order.

'It won't take long,' he said when he sat back at the table.

'Good. I am *starving*.'

'I'm not surprised after that workout you did.'

'It doesn't help that I forgot to have any dinner before we left.'

'How can you *forget* a meal?' He looked at her as if she'd confessed to forgetting to put her underwear on.

She shrugged. 'It happens. If I'm concentrating and lost in the music it is easy for me to forget.'

'It's no wonder you're a slip of thing.'

'I make up for it,' she said defensively. 'I might not eat at regular times, but I always eat.'

He eyed her, his look contemplative. Before he could say whatever was on his mind their food was brought over by yet another teenager.

'That *was* quick,' Amalie marvelled. Her famished belly rumbled loudly as she looked at the heaped plate. She didn't think she'd ever seen so many chips on a plate, or a burger of such epic proportions.

'We run a tight ship here.'

'That's not the first time you've said "we",' she said, picking up a thick golden chip that was so hot she dropped it back onto the plate. 'Are you involved in this place somehow?'

'This is my gym.'

She gazed at him, trying to stop her face wrinkling in puzzlement. 'But you have a gym in your villa.'

'And there's one at the palace too.' He picked up his burger and bit into it, devouring almost a quarter in one huge mouthful.

She shook her head. 'So why this place too?'

He swallowed, his light brown eyes on hers. 'This is a boxing gym. Sparring is no fun when you're on your own.'

'So you bought a gym so you could have some company?'

'There were a lot of reasons.'

'Do you run it?'

'I employ a manager. Enough questions—eat before your food gets cold.'

'Okay, but do me a favour and never tell my mother what I'm about to eat.'

His brow furrowed. 'Why? Would she disapprove?'

Amalie had already bitten into a chip, possibly the crispest and yet fluffiest chip she had ever tasted. She chewed, then swallowed it down with some Coke before answering. 'My mother is a gastronomy snob. She considers any food with English or American origin to be tantamount to eating out of a rubbish bin.'

'Yet she married an Englishman.'

'That's true,' she agreed, casting her eyes down. Her parents had been divorced for half her lifetime, yet the guilt still had the power to catch her unawares.

Talos picked up on an inflection in her tone. 'Was it a bad divorce?'

'Not at all. It was very civilised.'

'But traumatic for you?'

'It wasn't the easiest of experiences,' she conceded, before picking up her burger and taking a small bite.

It was with some satisfaction that he saw her eyes widen and her nod of approval.

'That is *good*,' she enthused when her mouth was clear.

'Maybe not the gastronomical heights your

mother would approve of, but still high-quality,' he agreed.

'I think this might be the best burger I've ever had.'

'You mean you've eaten a burger *before*?' he asked, feigning surprise. 'Your mother will be shocked.'

'I hide all my convenience food when I know she's coming over.'

He grinned and took another bite of his burger. The workout had clearly done Amalie the world of good; most of her primness had been sweated out of her. She almost looked relaxed.

They ate in silence for a few minutes. It gratified him to see her eat so heartily; he had imagined from her slender frame and self-confessed lack of exercise that she would eat like a sparrow.

He tried to imagine eating with another woman here and came up blank.

In normal life this gym was his sanctuary— not somewhere he would bring a date, even if his date liked to work out. For the same reason he refused to make overtures to any of the women who worked here. Regardless of the fact that most of his female staff were, like the majority of his employees, teenagers, and so automatically off limits, he didn't want the messiness that inevitably came about when he ended a relationship to spill into his sanctuary.

Melina, his kickboxing instructor, had blatantly flirted with him when she'd first started work here and—despite her being in her mid-twenties, and attractive to boot—he'd frozen out all her innuendoes until she'd got the message.

The endorphins released during a vigorous workout always made him crave sex, but he disciplined himself with the iron will Kalliakis men were famed for. Except for his father. The Kalliakis iron will had skipped a generation with Lelantos... Lelantos had been weak and venal—a man who had allowed his strong libido and equally great temper to control him.

It *killed* Talos to know that of the three Kalliakis Princes, he was the most like their father.

The difference was that he had learned to control his appetites *and* the volatile temperament that came with it. Boxing had taught him to harness it.

Tonight, though, the endorphins seemed to have exploded within him, and the primal urge to sate himself in a willing woman's arms was stronger than ever. And not just any woman. *This* woman.

Theos, just watching Amalie eat made him feel

like throwing her over his shoulder, carrying her to the nearest empty room and taking her wildly.

'Do you consider yourself French or English?' he asked, wrenching his mind away from matters carnal. He needed to concentrate on getting her mentally fit to play at his grandfather's gala, not be imagining ripping her clothes off with his teeth.

'Both. Why?'

'You speak English with a slight accent. It made me curious.'

'I suppose French is my first language. I grew up bilingual, but I've never lived full-time in England. My father's always kept a home there, but when I was a child we used it more for holidays and parties than anything else.'

'Was that because of your mother's influence?'

'I assume so. My mother definitely wore the trousers in that marriage.' A slight smile, almost sad, played at the corners of her lips.

'I have heard that she's a forceful woman.'

He'd heard many stories about Colette Barthez, not many of them complimentary. It was strange to think that the woman before him—a woman who tried desperately to fade into the background—was a child from the loins of the biggest diva on the planet. He had to assume she took after her father who, he'd learned, was regarded as a quintessential Englishman, with a dry humour and calm manner.

Amalie chewed on a chip, disliking the implication in his words and the way he'd delivered them. She, better than anyone, knew just how 'forceful' her mother could be in getting her own way, but that didn't stop her loving her and despising the people who would put her down.

'You don't become the most successful and famous mezzo-soprano in the world without having a strong will and a thick hide. If she were a man she would be celebrated.'

The scarred eyebrow rose in question.

She shook her head and pushed her plate to the side. 'She sold out Carnegie Hall and the Royal Albert Hall three nights in a row last year, but every article written about those concerts just *had* to mention her three ex-husbands, numerous lovers and so-called diva demands.'

The black scarred brow drew forward. 'That must be very hurtful for her to read,' he said, his tone careful.

'If it was the French media it would devastate her, but in France she's revered and treated as a national icon. With the rest of the world's press, so long as they aren't criticising her voice or performance, she doesn't care—she truly does have the hide of a rhinoceros.'

But not when it came to love. When it came to affairs of the heart, her mother felt things deeply. Bored lovers had the power to shatter her.

'But they upset *you*?' he said, a shrewdness in his eyes.

'No one wants to read salacious stories about their mother,' she muttered, reaching for one more chip and popping it in her mouth before she could unloosen her tongue any further.

Her family and personal life were none of his concern, but she felt so protective when it came to her mother, who was passionate, funny, loving, predatory, egotistical and a complete one-off. She drove her up the wall, but Amalie adored her.

'That is true,' Talos agreed. 'My family also live under the spotlight. There are occasions when it can burn.'

She leaned back in her chair and stared at him through narrowed eyes. 'If you know how much the spotlight can burn, why would you push me back under it when you know it hurts me so much?'

'Because you were born to play under it,' he replied, his deep bass voice no-nonsense.

And yet she detected a whisper of warmth in those light brown eyes she hadn't seen before.

'It is my job to put you back under it without you gaining any new scars.'

'But the scars I already have haven't healed.'

There was no point in shying away from it. She'd seen enough psychologists in her early teens to know that she'd been scarred, and that it was those scars still preventing her from stepping onto a stage and performing with eyes upon her.

'Then I will heal them for you.'

A shiver ran through her as an image of his mouth drifting across her skin skittered into her mind, shockingly vivid… Talos healing her in the most erotic manner. It sent a pulse of heat deep into her abdomen.

She blinked rapidly, to dispel the unbidden image, and was grateful when another member of the gym chose that moment to come over to their table and chat with him.

Passion was something she'd always avoided. After her parents' divorce she'd spent her weekend and holiday visitations watching her mother bounce from lover to lover, marrying two of them for good measure, engulfed in desire's heady flames, trying to recapture the magic of her first marriage. Watching her get burned so many times had been pain itself. The guilt of knowing she was responsible for her mother's heartache—and her father's—had only added to it.

Her father had never brought another woman home, let alone remarried. Though he would always deny it with a sad smile, the torch he carried for her mother was too bright to extinguish.

If it hadn't been for that horrendous incident in front of her parents and their friends and its aftermath, when their child prodigy could no longer perform like the dancing seal she'd become, her parents would still be together today—she was certain of it. On the occasions when they were forced together, Amalie would watch them skirt around each other; her mother showing off her latest lover with something close to flamboyant desperation, her father accepting this behaviour with a wistful stoicism.

Amalie *liked* her quiet, orderly, passionless life. It was safe.

Talos Kalliakis made her feel anything but safe.

Talos rapped loudly on the cottage door for the second time, blowing out a breath of exasperated air. Just as he was about to try the handle and let himself in the door swung open and there Amalie stood, violin in hand and a look of startled apology on her face.

'Is it that time already?' she said, standing aside to let him through. 'Sorry, I lost track of time.'

He followed her through to the cosy living room. The baby grand piano sat in the corner, covered with sheets of paper and an old-fashioned tape recorder. Next to it stood a music stand.

She looked what could only be described as lively—as if she had springs under her feet. In the four days she'd been in Agon he'd never seen her like this.

'Would you mind if I give the workout a miss tonight?' she asked, her green sapphire eyes vibrant and shining. 'I've reached an understanding with the score and I want to solidify it in my mind before I lose the moment.'

'You are making headway?' It amused him to hear her discussing the score as if it were a living entity.

'Something has clicked today. I've made a recording of the piano accompaniment—I am so grateful your grandmother wrote an accompaniment for the piano as well as for a full orchestra—and playing along to it is making all the pieces come together.'

'Are you ready to play it for me?'

Her eyes rounded in horror. 'Absolutely *not*.'

'You're going to have to play it for me soon,' he reminded her. The countdown was on, the gala only three weeks and six days away.

'Let me master the composition before we discuss that.'

He eyed her contemplatively. 'You have until Friday.'

She'd accompanied him to his gym three nights in a row, her workouts intense and focused. Wanting her concentration to be used in figuring out the score, he'd deliberately steered any small talk between them away from the personal. Other than chauffeuring her to and from the gym, he'd left her to it.

A dart of panic shot from her eyes. 'I won't be ready by Friday.'

'Friday will give us three weeks to get you performance-ready. I know nothing of music. It makes no difference to me if you make mistakes at this early stage; I won't notice them. What concerns me is getting you used to playing solo in front of people again. We need to work on that as much as you need to work on the score itself.'

A mutinous expression flashed over her face before her features relaxed a touch and she nodded.

'You can have tonight off, but tomorrow you go back to the gym.'

'Has anyone ever told you that you're a slave-driving ogre?'

'No one has dared.'

She rolled her eyes. 'I want to get on—you can leave now.'

'And no one has ever dared tell me when I should leave before.'

'You must be getting old, because your memory is failing—I've told you to leave before, at my home in Paris when you barged your way in.'

'Ah, yes. I distinctly remember you tried using physical force to expel me.'

His loins tightened as memories of her soft, lithe body splayed on his lap while he controlled the flare of fire and passion that had exploded out of her assailed him anew. He cast a long, appreciative look up and down her body, taking in the short black skirt over sheer black tights and the short-sleeved viridian-green shirt unbuttoned to display a hint of cleavage…

'Would you like to use force to expel me now?'

She cuddled her violin to her chest as if for protection and took a step back.

'Imagine how fit all those workouts will make you,' he purred in a deliberately sensual tone, enjoying the colour heightening her cheekbones. 'Next time you choose to fight me with your body you might have a chance of overpowering me.'

'We both know I could train twenty-four hours a day, every day for a decade, and still not be strong enough to overpower you.'

'If you would like to put that theory into practice you only have to say.' He dropped his voice and stared straight into her almond eyes. *Theos*, she was temptation itself. 'I'm not averse to a beautiful woman trying to dominate me. Something tells me the results would be explosive.'

Other than the colour on her face, she showed no reaction. For the briefest of moments Talos wondered if his assumption that the attraction he felt for her was mutual was wrong—then he saw her swallow and swipe a lock of hair from her forehead.

'Enjoy your music,' he said, stepping out of the room with one last grin.

As he shut the cottage front door behind him he ruefully conceded that trying to get a rise out of the beautiful musician living in his guest house had served no purpose other than to fuel the chemistry swirling between them.

He would need an extra-long workout to expel the energy fizzing in his veins.

CHAPTER SIX

AMALIE DID SOMETHING SACRILEGIOUS. In a fit of temper, she threw the precious score onto the floor.

Immediately she felt wretched. It wasn't the poor score's fault that all the good feelings that had grown throughout the day had vanished. It was the composer's rotten grandson who had caused that with his rotten innuendoes.

Focus, Amalie, she told herself sternly.

But it was hard to focus on the sheets of wonderful music before her when all she could think about was wrestling Talos's clothes off him and seeing for herself if he was as divine naked as he was when clothed.

That body…

It would be hard. Every inch of it. But what would his skin feel like? Would it be hard too? Or would it be smooth? How would it feel against her own skin?

Focus!

It was none of her business what Talos Kalliakis's

skin felt like, or how hard his body was, or to discover if it was true that the size of a man's feet was proportionate to the size of his...

Focus!

Talos had enormous feet. And enormous hands...

He also had a smile that churned her belly into soft butter.

'Stop it!' This time she shouted the words aloud and clenched her fists.

She'd woken that morning with a sense of dread that the gala was now less than four weeks away. If she didn't master the composition, then it didn't matter what tricks Talos had up his sleeve to get her performing onstage—she would be humiliated regardless. Right at that moment all that mattered was the composition.

Sitting herself on the floor, she hitched her skirt to the top of her thighs, crossed her legs and closed her eyes. There she sat for a few minutes, concentrating on nothing but her breathing—a technique taught to her by her father, who had confessed in a conspiratorial manner that it was the breathing technique her mother had learnt when she'd been in labour with Amalie. By all accounts her mother had ignored the midwife's advice and demanded more drugs.

The thought brought a smile to her face and pulled her out of the trance-like state she'd slipped into.

The edginess that had consumed her since Talos's brief visit had subsided a little, enough for her to put the sheets of music back onto her stand and press 'play' on the tape recorder.

As she waited for the backing music to begin she couldn't help thinking she *should* have gone for a workout, which would have cleared her angst so much better than any meditation technique.

She nestled her violin under her chin and as the first notes of the accompaniment played out she counted the beats and began to play.

Soon she was immersed in the music, so much so that when a loud rap on the front door echoed through to the living room she had to physically pull herself out of it. A quick glance at her watch showed she'd been playing for two and a half hours.

She yanked the door open just as Talos raised his knuckles for another rap.

'Have you never heard the word *patience* before?' she scolded.

He grinned and held up a large cardboard box, the motion causing a warm waft of scent to emit from it. 'I'm too hungry for patience, little song-bird. I bring us food.'

Us?

The divine smell triggered something in her belly, making it rumble loudly. With a start she realised she'd forgotten to eat the tray of food a member of his villa's staff had brought to the cottage for her earlier that evening.

Since their first trip to his gym, lunch and dinner had been brought to her on Talos's orders. She knew it was only the fear that she would become anaemic or something, and faint from hunger onstage, that prompted him to do it, rather than any regard for *her*, but his concern touched her nonetheless.

The tray from earlier was still on the dining table, untouched. A warm, almost fluffy feeling trickled through her blood that he'd noticed.

Hesitating for only a moment, she let him in and headed to the kitchen, grabbed a couple of plates and some cutlery, and took them through to the dining area of the living room.

What was she supposed to do? Insist that he leave when he'd gone to the trouble of bringing her food, just because she kept having erotic thoughts about him? It would be incredibly rude. He might have used blackmail to get her here, but since then he'd treated her decently. He'd treated her well. Thoughtfully. She wasn't a prisoner, as she'd feared she would be, but had his whole household staff at her disposal for whatever she wanted or needed.

More than any of that, she would be spending a *lot* more time with him in the coming weeks. She had to get used to feeling off-centre when she was with him. She *had* to. She refused to become a gibbering idiot in his presence.

Talos held aloft a bottle of rosé retsina. 'Glasses?'

Once they were settled at the table, Talos busy removing the foil lids of the dozen boxes spread out before them, she said, 'I didn't think there would be any takeaways open on a Sunday night.'

One of the chattier members of Talos's staff had warned her yesterday to get anything she needed on Saturday, as the island mostly shut down on a Sunday.

'There aren't—I got the chefs at the palace to cook for us.'

Oh, yes. He was a prince. In Paris his royalty was something she'd been acutely aware of. Here, in the relaxed atmosphere of Agon, it was an easy thing to forget.

'And they have proper takeaway boxes to hand?'

'The palace kitchens are ten times the size of this cottage and cater for all eventualities,' he answered lightly, pouring the retsina.

'Didn't you go to the gym?' He'd showered and changed into a pair of black chinos and a dark blue polo shirt since he'd turned up at the cottage earlier, so he'd clearly done his workout, but she couldn't see how he'd have had time to go the gym *and* the palace in the short time he'd been gone.

'As you weren't doing the kickboxing class I worked out at the palace gym. It gave me a chance to catch up with my brothers and my grandfather.'

That would be the King and the two other Kalliakis Princes.

'I thought you went to your gym every night?'

'I work out every night, but not always at the gym. I try and make it there a couple of times a week when I'm in the country.'

'Have you been putting yourself out for *me*, then?'

'You're my current project,' he said with a wolfish grin. 'As long as I get you on that stage for the gala I don't care if I have to be inconvenienced.'

That was right. She was his pet project. She had to remember that anything nice he did was with an ulterior motive and not for *her*.

She took a sip of retsina, expecting to grimace at the taste, which she'd always found rather harsh. It was surprisingly mellow—like an expensive white wine but with that unmistakable resinous tang.

'You approve?' he asked.

She nodded.

'Good. It is our island's vintage.'

'Do you make it?'

'No—we rent out our land to a producer who makes it under the island's own label.'

The food looked and tasted as divine as its aroma. Amalie happily dived into *kleftiko*—the most tender slow-cooked lamb on the bone she'd ever eaten—and its accompanying *yemista*—stuffed baked tomatoes and peppers—eating as much as she could fit into her stomach. She hadn't realised how hungry she was.

As during their shared meal at his gym, Talos ate heartily. When he'd finished wolfing down every last scrap on his plate, and emptying the takeaway boxes of every last morsel, he stuck his fork into the few leftovers on her plate.

'For a prince, you don't behave in a very regal fashion,' she observed drily.

'How is a prince supposed to behave?'

She considered, before answering, 'Regally?'

He burst into laughter—a deep, booming sound that filled the small cottage. 'I leave the regal behaviour to my brothers.'

'How do you get away with that?'

'They're the heir and the spare.' He raised a hefty shoulder into a shrug. 'Helios will take over the throne when my grandfather...'

Here, his words faltered—just a light falter, that anyone who wasn't observing him closely would likely have missed. But she *was* observing him closely—was unable to tear her eyes away from him. It wasn't just the magnetic sex appeal he oozed. The more time she spent with him, the more he fascinated her. The man behind the magnetism.

'When the day comes,' he finished smoothly. 'Theseus has been groomed for the role too, for the remote eventuality that something untoward should happen to Helios.' He must have caught her shock at his unemotional analysis because he added, 'No one knows what's around the corner. Our father was heir to the throne, but life threw a curveball at him when he was only a couple of years older than I am now.'

The car crash. The tragedy that had befallen the Kalliakis family a quarter of a century before, leaving the three young Princes orphaned. Looking at the huge man sitting opposite her, she found it was almost impossible to imagine Talos as a small child. But he had been once, and had suffered the most horrendous thing that could happen to any child: the death of not one but both parents.

The sudden temptation to cover his giant hand and whisper her sympathies was smothered by the equally sudden hard warning in his eyes—a look impossible to misinterpret. *I do not want your sympathies. This subject is not open to discussion.*

Instead she said, 'Did your brothers get favourable treatment?'

He relaxed back immediately into a grin. 'Not at all. *I* got all the preferential treatment. I was the happy accident. I was raised without any expectations—a prince in a kingdom where the most that is expected of me is to protect my brothers if ever the need arises. Even my name denotes that. In ancient mythology Talos was a giant man of bronze. There are a number of differing myths about him, but the common theme is that he was a protector.'

Goosebumps broke out over her flesh.

Something told her this big brute of a man would be a fierce protector—and not simply because of his physique.

Cross him or those he loved and you would know about it.

She cleared her throat. 'Aren't older siblings supposed to protect the youngest, not the other way round?'

His smile broadened. 'Usually. But I was such a large newborn my parents knew my role would be to protect my brothers from anyone who would do harm to them or our lands.'

'And have you had to do much in the way of protection?' she asked.

'When I was a child it seemed my role was to protect them from each other,' he said with another laugh. 'They used to fight constantly. We all did.'

'Do you get on now?'

'We all still fight, but nowadays it is only verbally. We are brothers, and we get on and work well together. We protect each other. That said, they are both big enough and ugly enough to take care of themselves.'

Amalie felt a pang of envy. She would have loved a sibling of her own. Any kind of playmate would have been wonderful. Anything would have been better than a childhood spent travelling the world with her parents on their various tours, educational tutors in tow, the only child in a world full of adults.

'Even so, aren't princes supposed to travel with a retinue of protectors at all times? And have lots of flunkeys?' In Paris he'd arrived at her home alone both times. And the only staff he'd brought to the Théâtre de la Musique had been clerical.

'It would take a very brave person to take me on—don't you think, little songbird?'

She felt her cheeks turn scarlet. She wished he would stop addressing her as *little songbird*— hated the rush of warmth that flushed through her whenever he called her it. Instinct told her that to acknowledge it would be like waving a red flag to a bull.

'Helios always travels with protection—Theseus less so.' Something sparked in his eyes, as if he were asking a question of himself. 'If you would like to see me behave in a more regal fashion you can accompany me to the ball at the palace next weekend.'

'What ball?'

'It's something Helios is hosting—a private pre-gala celebration. There will be royal flunkeys and footmen everywhere, princes and princesses from around the world—and I, little songbird, will be in my most princely attire.'

'And you want me to go with you?' Was he asking her to go as his *date*?

'It will give me a chance to show you how princely I really am,' he teased.

'If it's such a formal affair, why haven't you already got someone to take with you?'

'If I took anyone else she would take it as a sign that I was serious about her and expect me to drop to one knee.'

'Do I take it that means you're not enamoured of the thought of marriage?'

Disgust crossed his face, as if she'd suggested he dunk his head into a vat of slime.

'You're a *prince*. Aren't you supposed to marry and produce heirs?'

'Helios will produce all the heirs Agon needs. Theseus will marry and produce some more as backup. Leaving me free to continue my bachelor lifestyle for eternity.'

'The eternal playboy?'

'I dislike that term,' he said, his eyes narrowing. 'It implies a certain disrespect towards women.'

She had to laugh. 'Don't tell me you're a feminist?'

'My grandmother was the strongest person I've ever known. If I was to disrespect any woman or make judgements on the basis of her gender I am

certain my grandmother would hunt me down in
my dreams to give me a dressing-down.'

'She sounds like a formidable woman.'

Talos nodded. Without his grandmother's loving
but steely influence—especially when he'd hit his
teenage years and gone completely off the rails—
he knew he wouldn't be half the man he was today.

'She was a pillar of strength,' he said, raising his
glass of retsina. 'And I think she would approve of
you playing her final composition.'

She made a snorting sound. 'Why would you
think that?'

'Because you have the same steel core she had.'

Amalie's eyes widened, and then she frowned, a
V forming in the centre of her brow. 'I can't perform in front of people. *My* core is made of blanc-
mange.'

'But, little songbird, you are the only person
other than my family who dares stand up to me.'

Even now she was disagreeing with him.

For the first time he understood why Theseus
had taken a two-year sabbatical after he'd completed his time at Sandhurst. The travelling part
he'd always understood, but Theseus's insistence
on travelling under an assumed name had been
something he'd never got. Talos was proud to be

a Kalliakis—proud of their family reputation as fighters, proud of his nation's people and culture. He saw himself as a protector of their proud island and had seen Theseus's insistence at disguising his identity as a snub to the Kalliakis name.

Now he understood how it must have felt for his brother to be treated as someone...*normal*. Theseus had shared many of his tales about the personal freedom he'd found in his time away, but only now did Talos understand why it had been such a special time for him.

Amalie was the first person since childhood to treat him like a normal person. She had no qualms about disagreeing with him on any subject. As he thought back over the past few days he realised that she simply didn't pander to him. He could be *anyone*.

Which meant that when she smiled at him— which, admittedly, was rarely—it was because she meant it. When those stunning green eyes became stark, their pupils enlarged, showing her desire for him—little tells she would hate to know he recognised—it was for *him*.

He'd never bedded a woman and been one hundred per cent certain whether she was in his arms out of desire for him or the aphrodisiac quality of his title. It had never bothered him—indeed, the idea that he could bed any woman he chose held an aphrodisiac quality of its own—but the mistrust had always been there, unacknowledged yet simmering away in the depths of his consciousness.

If he were to make love to Amalie there was no question that her responses would be authentic. If she made love to him it would be for *him*.

The temptation to lean over the table, cup that beautiful heart-shaped chin in his hand and taste those delectable lips was so strong he dug his toes into his boots to keep his feet grounded to the floor.

Theos, it was a temptation that grew harder to resist the more time he spent with her. His will power and control were legendary, and yet he was having to remind himself of all the reasons he had to hone them to greater strengths when with this woman.

Making love to Amalie could be disastrous. He was supposed to be getting her fit to play at his grandfather's gala, not plotting to get those lithe limbs wrapped around his waist…

He looked at his watch and got sharply to his feet. 'I need to head back. I'm flying to New York in the morning but I'll be back Thursday evening.

I'll get Kostas to take you to Natalia's—she'll make a ball dress for you.'

'I haven't agreed to come,' she protested.

'I am a prince of the land, little songbird,' he answered with a grin. 'If you defy my wishes I will have you locked in the palace dungeons.'

'You've already said the dungeons are only a tourist attraction.'

He winked at her. 'It will take me two minutes to appropriate the keys for them.'

He laughed at the scowl she bestowed upon him.

'I'll see myself out. *Kali nýchta*, little songbird.'

He might not have any intention of acting on the absurdly strong chemistry growing between them, but he could damn well enjoy her company for one evening of entertainment.

CHAPTER SEVEN

A LOUD RAP on the front door broke Amalie out of the spell she was under.

She froze, violin under her chin, bow bouncing lightly on the E string. There was only one person she knew who so vividly announced his presence with just a knock on the door.

The five days of peace without Talos had come to an end. He'd returned to Agon the previous evening but she'd had a lucky escape in that he hadn't bothered with her. That hadn't stopped her spending the entire evening at his gym, looking over her shoulder, waiting for him to appear. And that sinking feeling when she'd been driven back to the cottage without him having made an appearance had *not* been disappointment.

'Hello, little songbird,' he said now, with a lazy smile on his face, the mid-afternoon sun shining down on him, enveloping him in a hazy, warm aura that made her stomach flip left, right and centre. 'Have you missed me?'

'Like a migraine,' she answered with a roll of her eyes, turning back into the cottage and leaving him to shut the door and follow her in, his low laughter at her quip reverberating through her.

'Have you had a good week?' he asked, stepping into the living room.

'It's been very peaceful, thank you. And yours?'

'Incredibly boring.'

'That'll teach you to be a lawyer.'

Today he actually looked lawyerly. Well, more like Tarzan dressed up as a lawyer, the crisp white shirt, open at the neck, rippling over his muscular chest, and charcoal trousers emphasising the length and power of his thighs. No matter what he wore he would still emit enough testosterone to fill a dozen buckets.

'It's a living,' he said, deadpan.

She couldn't help it. She laughed. She doubted Talos Kalliakis had needed to work a single day in his life.

'What does a man have to do to get a coffee round here?' he asked.

'Go to the kitchen and work the coffee machine.'

'But I am royalty. I shouldn't be expected to make my own coffee.'

'I'll have a mocha while you're there,' she said, only just stopping herself throwing a wink at him.

His irreverence was contagious.

His nose wrinkled. 'I have serious doubts about your taste, knowing you drink that muck.'

She had serious doubts about her taste too. Always she'd steered herself in the direction of safe, dependable men, those with whom she could have a nice, safe, dependable life.

There was nothing *safe* about Talos.

That little fact didn't stop her thinking about him constantly.

It didn't stop her heart from hammering at a *prestissimo* pace by virtue of just being under the same roof as him.

Luckily he took himself off to the kitchen, allowing her a few minutes to compose herself. When he returned, carrying their coffees, she'd put her violin away and sat herself in an armchair.

He placed their cups on the table and sprawled onto the sofa. 'I hear you've been going to the gym every day.'

'I was under orders, remember?'

He grinned. 'Melina thinks it is a shame you can't actually fight someone in a kickboxing match.'

Likely Melina would volunteer herself for that honour. Whilst not unfriendly, there was a definite coolness in the instructor's attitude towards her.

'I enjoy it,' she admitted.

The atmosphere at Talos's gym was different from anything she'd experienced before. There was a real collective feel about it, with everyone there prepared to help everyone else. Yes, there were some big egos, but it was a different kind of egotism from the sort she was used to in the classical music world—earthier, somehow. Considering she was one of the only women there, she never felt threatened, and she didn't think it was because everyone knew she was Talos's guest. The atmosphere of the gym itself engendered respect in all its patrons.

'Good. And how are you getting on with the score?'

'Well...I think.'

He quirked his scarred brow. 'You *think*?'

'I have no way of knowing if I'm playing it as your grandmother intended.'

'How do you mean?'

'My interpretation of the tempo she played it at might be different from her interpretation.'

He shrugged. 'You played the "Méditation" from

Thaïs at a slower tempo than she played it, but it sounded equally beautiful.'

Talos noted the colour flush over her face, the flash of embarrassed pride that darted from her eyes.

He sat forward and rested his arms on his thighs. 'It is time for you to play for me.'

Her colour faded as quickly as it had appeared. She seemed to cower in her seat.

'I did say I would listen to you play today.'

She brightened. 'I've recorded myself playing it. You can listen to that.'

He cocked his head and sighed theatrically. 'I can see that working well at the gala—we'll introduce our star soloist and wheel on a tape recorder with a wig.'

She spluttered a sound of nervous laughter.

He softened his voice, wanting to put her at ease. 'It is only you and me. It doesn't matter how many mistakes you make—all that matters is that today you play for me.'

There were three weeks and one day until the gala.

Judging by the terror vibrating off Amalie's frame, he would need every one of them.

He'd spent the four days in New York getting as

much work done as he could, organising his staff and generally ensuring that he'd need to do minimal travelling until the gala was over. The business was being neglected by all three Kalliakis princes but what alternative did they have? All of them wanted to spend as much time with their grandfather as they could, to be there when he was having a good spell and craving their company. They were fortunate that their staff were the best of the best and could run much of the business with minimum input from them.

This trip away had been different from any other. He was always impatient to spend as much time on Agon as he could, but during this trip he'd found himself thinking of home far more frequently than normal. Thinking of *her* in his little guest cottage. He'd arrived back early yesterday evening and the temptation to pay her an immediate visit had shocked him with its intensity.

He'd resisted and headed to the palace. There, he'd shared a meal with his brothers, both of whom had been in foul tempers and had declined to answer any questions about their respective bad moods. Both had excused themselves the moment they'd finished eating. Shrugging his shoulders at their odd behaviour, Talos had sought out his grandfather, spending a pleasant couple of hours playing chess with him until a sudden bout of tiredness had forced his grandfather to call a halt.

It unnerved him how quickly his grandfather could fall into exhaustion—one minute sitting upright, laughing, holding a conversation; the next his chin drooping, his eyes struggling to stay open, his speech slurring...

Talos could feel the time ebbing away. He could see it too. He'd only been four days in New York and his grandfather had lost even more weight, the large, vital man now a shadow of his former self.

The woman before him had the power to make his grandfather's last days the sweetest they could be. She could bring his beloved Rhea's final composition to life. She was the only person in the world who could do it justice.

He watched Amalie struggle for composure, feeling a strange tugging in his chest when she visibly forced herself to her feet and over to the baby grand piano, where she'd left her violin.

Not looking at him, she removed it from its case and fiddled with the strings, tuning them as his grandmother had always done before playing for him.

Moving her music stand behind the piano, as if

she were using the piano for protection, she arranged the sheets of music until she was satisfied with how they stood, then rested her violin under her chin.

About to hit the first note, she halted, bow upright, and stared at him. 'I've almost memorised it. I won't need the sheet music when I do the gala.'

It was the first time he'd heard her utter her intentions to actually perform at the gala. He wondered if she was aware of what she'd just given away—how in the nine days she had been on his island her mind-set had already altered.

He raised his hands and pulled a face to indicate his nonchalance about such matters. What did he care if she played with the music in front of her or not? All he cared was that she played it.

'I'll play without the accompaniment.'

'Stop stalling and *play.*'

She swallowed and nodded, then closed her eyes.

Her bow struck the first note.

And bounced off the string.

He watched her closely. The hand holding the violin—the hand with the short nails, which he suddenly realised were kept that length to stop them inadvertently hitting the strings when playing—was holding the instrument in a death grip.

The hand holding the bow was shaking. It came to him in flash why her nails seemed so familiar. His grandmother had kept her nails in the same fashion.

'Take some deep breaths,' he instructed, hooking an ankle over his knee, making sure to keep his tone low and unthreatening.

She gave a sharp nod and, eyes still closed, inhaled deeply through her nose.

It made no difference. The bow bounced off the strings again.

She breathed in again.

The same thing happened.

'What are you thinking of right now?' he asked after a few minutes had passed, the only sound the intermittent bounce of her bow on the strings whenever she made another attempt to play. Her distress was palpable. 'What's in your head?'

'That I feel naked.'

Her eyes opened and blinked a couple of times before fixing on him. Even with Amalie at the other end of the room he could see the starkness in her stare.

'Do you ever have that dream where you go somewhere and are surrounded by people doing ordinary things, and you look down and discover you have *nothing* on?'

'I am aware of people having those dreams,' he conceded, although it wasn't one he'd personally experienced.

No, *his* dreams—nightmares—were infinitely darker, his own powerlessness represented by having to relive that last evening with his parents, when he'd jumped onto his father's back and pounded at him with his little fists.

His father had bucked him off with such force that he'd clattered to the floor and hit his head on the corner of their bed. In his dreams he had to relive his mother holding him in her arms, soothing him, kissing his sore, bleeding head and wiping away his tears which had mingled with her own.

It was the last time he'd seen them.

He hadn't been allowed to see them when they'd lain in state. The condition of their bodies had been so bad that closed caskets had been deemed the only option.

And that was the worst of his nightmares—when he would walk into the family chapel and lift the lids of their coffins to see the ravages the car crash had wreaked on them. His imagination in those nightmares was limitless…

'Try and imagine it, because it's the closest I can come to explaining how I feel right now,' she said, her voice as stark as the panic in her eyes.

For the first time he believed—*truly* believed—that her fear was genuine. He'd always believed it was real, but had assumed she'd been exaggerating for effect.

This was no exaggeration.

'You feel naked?' he asked evenly. He, more than anyone, knew how the imagination could run amok, the fear of the unknown so much worse than reality. He also knew how he could help her take the first step to overcome it.

'Yes,' she whispered.

The strange distance Amalie had seen settling over him had dissipated, and his attention on her was focused and strong.

'Then there is only one solution. You must *be* naked.'

'What…?'

But her solitary word hardly made it past her vocal cords. Talos had leant forward and was pulling his shoes and socks off.

What was he doing?

His hands went to his shirt. Before she could

comprehend what she was seeing he'd deftly undone all the buttons.

'What are you doing?'

He got to his feet.

If she hadn't already pressed herself against the
wall she would have taken a step back. She would
have turned and run.

But there was nowhere for her to run *to*—not
without getting past him first.

'The only way you're going to overcome your
fear of nakedness is to *play* naked.'

His tone was calm, at complete odds with the
panic careering through her.

She could not dislodge her tongue from the roof
of her mouth.

He shrugged his arms out of his shirt and hung
it on the back of a dining chair.

His torso was magnificent, broad and muscular, his skin a golden bronze. A light smattering
of black hair covered his defined pecs, somehow
tempering the muscularity.

As nonchalant as if he were undressing alone for
a shower, he tugged at the belt of his trousers, then
undid the button and pulled the zip down.

'Please, stop,' she beseeched him.

He fixed her with a stare that spoke no nonsense,

then pulled his trousers down, taking his underwear with them. Stepping out of them, he folded and placed them over his shirt, then propped himself against the wall, his full attention back on her.

'I am not going to force you to take your clothes off,' he said, in that same deep, calm tone. 'But if you play naked for me now you will have lived out your worst fear and in the process you will have overcome it. I would not have you at the disadvantage of being naked alone so I have removed my clothes to put us on an equal footing. I will stay here, where I stand. You have my word that I will not take a step closer to you. Unless,' he added with the wolfish grin she was becoming familiar with, 'you ask me to.'

All she could do was shake her head mutely, but not with the terror he was reading in her, but because she'd been rendered speechless.

She'd known Talos naked would be a sight to behold, but she had never dreamed how magnificent he would be.

Why him? she wondered desperately.

Why did her body choose *this* man to respond to?

Why did it have to respond at all?

She knew what desire looked like, had seen her mother in its grip so many times, then seen her heart broken as her most recent lover tired of the incessant diva demands and ended things, shattering her mother's heart and fragile ego.

Passion and its companion desire were dangerous things she wanted no part of, had shied away from since early adolescence. Hearts were made to be broken, and it was desire that pulled you into its clutches.

All those protections she'd placed around her libido and sense of self were crumbling.

Talos's grin dropped. 'I said I would help you, little songbird, but you have to help yourself too. You have to take the first step.'

Her breaths were coming so hard she could feel the air expanding her lungs.

She thought frantically. She hadn't ever shown her naked body to a man before. Her few boyfriends had never put pressure on her, respecting her need to wait, the lie she'd told them in order to defer any kind of physicality. Kind men. *Safe* men.

Was it the safety she'd sought that had kept alive her fear of performing?

One of her psychiatrists—the most astute of them all—had once said he didn't believe she *wanted* to be fixed. She'd denied it but now, looking back, she considered the possibility that he'd been partly right.

Her life was *safe*. Maybe a little boring, but she'd found her niche and she never wanted to leave it or the emotional protection it gave her.

But she had to. She couldn't stay there any longer. If she didn't step out she would lose that little niche anyway—for good. Her job would be gone. Her income would be gone. Her independence would be gone. All her friends' lives would be destroyed too.

'We are more alike than you think, you and I,' Talos said.

His voice was deeper and lower than she had ever heard it, every syllable full of meaning. He still hadn't made a move towards her.

'We have both chosen solitary pursuits. I focus on my boxing, you have your violin. No one can pull my punches for me and no one can play that violin for you. Think of the emotions you get when you're kickboxing, the adrenaline you feel through your veins. *That* is how you must imagine your fear—as something to be channelled and fought. You are on Agon, the land of warriors. We fight. And so must you. *Fight*, little songbird. Loosen your hold and *fly*.'

She gripped onto the piano for support and closed her eyes, his words resonating through her.

Was it time to confront all the fear?

If not now, then when?

If not here, then where?

'Will you turn around when I undress?'

'I will, but when you play I will watch you. I cannot guarantee I will stop my thoughts roaming to inappropriate places, but I *can* guarantee I will not act on them.'

I wish I could guarantee the same.

'If you can get through this you can get through anything. I give you my word.'

Strike her down, but she believed him.

'Right here and now it is you and me—no one else. If you make mistakes then keep going. You can do this, Amalie.'

Whether it was the calm sincerity in his voice or the confidence emanating from him—God, he was *naked*—something worked, turning the panic inside her down low enough for her to get a grip on herself.

'Please turn around,' she said shakily.

He did as she asked, standing so his back was to her. His back was every bit as beautiful as his front, his body a mass of taut muscle and sinew.

He was not professional-body-builder big, but big enough that you would trust him to pull a car off a helpless victim and then carry them over his shoulder to safety without breaking a sweat.

With fingers that fumbled she pulled off her pretty blue top and shrugged her skirt down. Her legs already bare, all that was left was her underwear. She tried to undo her bra, but what was second nature suddenly became the hardest job in the world.

'I *can't*,' she said, suddenly panic-stricken all over again.

Talos turned his head a touch before twisting his whole body round. Arms folded across his chest, he gazed at her, the look on his face something she'd never seen before. It looked as if it hurt him to breathe.

'That is enough,' he said quietly. 'Now, please— play for me.'

This time she allowed her eyes to dart down and look at what she'd tried to keep as a haze, skimming around the area as if it were pixilated.

The heat that rushed through her at one glance almost knocked her off her feet.

The knowing look that came into his eyes had the same effect.

Talos was in proportion in *every* way.

Suddenly she yanked her violin off the piano, put it under chin and began to play.

The bow swept across the strings, bouncing gently because of her less than graceful start, but then it did what it had been made to do, whilst her fingers flew up and down the strings. It was probably the worst start to a performance she'd ever given, but she wouldn't have known either way as at that moment she wasn't hearing the music, but simply relishing the fact that she was winning this fight. She was doing it. She was playing in front of someone.

God, she was virtually *naked*.

And Talos was as naked as the day he'd been born.

Somehow she settled into the music, embraced it, letting it become her. Far from closing her eyes, she kept her gaze on him, felt the heat of his returning stare.

By the time she played the last note the tension in the room had merged with the vibrato of her violin, a tangible, pulsating chemistry she felt all the way through to her core.

For long, long moments nothing was said. Not verbally.

The connection between their gazes spoke a thousand words.

'You brought my skin up in bumps,' he finally said, his voice raspy.

She gave a helpless shrug.

'You didn't play my grandmother's composition.'

She shook her head. She had played the final movement of one of Vivaldi's *Four Seasons* concertos—'Summer'. The movement that evoked a thunderstorm and perfectly fitted the storm raging beneath her skin.

'I didn't want you to hear it when I knew I wouldn't be able to do it justice. Not the first time.'

'The first time should be special, yes.'

She breathed deeply, sensing he wasn't talking about the music any more.

He made no move towards her. The look in his eyes was clear. He'd made her a promise not to get any closer to her. Not unless she invited him to.

Her blood had never felt so thick, as if she'd had hot treacle injected into her veins.

She wanted him. Desperately. Passionately…

No!

The warning shout in her head rang out loud and clear, breaking through the chemistry buffeting them, shattering it with one unsaid syllable.

Without a word she grabbed her top and pulled it back on, smoothing it over her belly as she darted a glance to see his reaction.

He inclined his head, an amused yet pained smile on his lips, then turned to his clothes and stepped back into his underwear and trousers before slipping his powerful arms into his shirt.

'You played beautifully, little songbird. And now it is time for me to leave.'

'Already?' The word escaped before she could catch it.

He dropped his stare down to his undone trousers. 'Unless you want me to break my promise?'

He cocked his head, waiting for an answer that wouldn't form.

'I thought not.' His eyes flashed. 'But we both know it's only a matter of time.'

She swallowed the moisture that had filled in her mouth, pushing it past the tightness in her throat.

'A car will collect you tomorrow at seven.'

'Seven?' she asked stupidly, her mind turning blank at his abrupt turn of conversation.

'Helios's ball,' he reminded her, fastening the last of his buttons. 'Did you receive the official invitation?'

She nodded. Her invitation had been hand delivered by a palace official, the envelope containing it a thick, creamy material, sealed with a wax insignia. Receiving it had made her feel like a princess from a bygone age.

'Keep it safe—you'll need to present it when you arrive. I'll be staying at my apartment in the palace for the weekend, so I'll send a car for you.'

She'd assumed they would travel there together, and was unnerved by the twinge of disappointment she felt at learning differently.

'Okay,' she answered, determined to mask the emotion.

It wasn't as if they were going on a proper date or anything, she reminded herself. She was simply his 'plus one' for the evening.

'Are you happy with your dress?' he asked.

On Monday Amalie had been driven by a member of Talos's staff to a pretty beachside house and introduced to an elegant elderly woman called Natalia. Natalia had measured every inch of her, clearly seizing her up as she did so. Then she had sat at her desk and sketched, spending less time than it took for Amalie to finish a coffee before she'd ripped the piece of paper off the pad and held out the rough but strangely intricate design to her.

'This is your dress,' she had said, with calm authority.

Amalie had left the house twenty minutes later with more excitement running through her veins than she had ever experienced before. She'd been to plenty of high-society parties in her lifetime, but never to a royal ball. And she was to wear a dress like *nothing* she had worn in her life. Natalia's vision had been so compelling and assured that she had rolled along with it, swept up in the designer's vision.

It was strange and unnerving to think she was to be the guest of a prince. She no longer thought of Talos in that light. Only as a man...

'Natalia is bringing it tomorrow so she can help me into it.' The dress fastening was definitely a two-person job. If the designer hadn't been coming to her Amalie would have had to find someone else to help her fasten it. She might have had to ask Talos to hook it for her...

He nodded his approval.

Dressed, Talos ran his fingers through his hair in what looked to Amalie like a futile attempt on his behalf to tame it.

There was nothing tameable about this man.

'Until tomorrow, little songbird,' he said, before letting himself out of the cottage.

Only when all the energy that followed him like a cloud had dissipated from the room did Amalie dare breathe properly.

With shaky legs she sat on the piano bench and pressed her face to the cool wood.

Maybe if she sat there for long enough the compulsion to chase after him and throw herself at him would dissipate too.

CHAPTER EIGHT

THE BLACK LIMOUSINE drove over a bridge and through a long archway before coming to a stop in a vast courtyard at the front of the palace.

Her heart fluttering madly beneath her ribs, Amalie stared in awe, just as she'd been gaping since she'd caught her first glimpse of it, magnificent and gleaming under the last red embers of the setting sun.

The driver opened the door for her and held out an arm, which she accepted gratefully. She had never worn heels so high. She had never felt so... *elegant.*

That's what wearing the most beautiful bespoke dress in creation does for you.

Still gaping, she stared up. The palace was so vast she had to make one-hundred-and-eighty-degree turns to see from one side to the next. Although vastly different in style, its romanticism rivalled France's beautiful Baroque palaces. Its architecture was a mixture of styles she'd seen throughout Europe and North Africa, forming its own unique and deeply beautiful style that resembled a great sultan's palace with gothic undertones.

Two dozen wide curved steps led up to a high-arched ornate entrance, where two footmen dressed in purple-and-gold livery with yellow sashes stood. She climbed the steps towards them, thinking that this was surely what Cinderella had felt like. After studiously checking her official invitation, another footman stepped forward to escort her into the palace itself.

First they entered a reception room so vast her entire cottage would fit inside it—roof and all, with room to spare—then walked through to another room where a group of footmen were being given last-minute instructions by a man who wore a red sash over his livery.

'Am I the first to arrive?' she asked her escort, who unfortunately spoke as much French and English as she spoke Greek—none at all.

It wasn't just the footmen being given instructions or the lack of other guests that made her think she was the first. Scores of waiting staff were also being given a last-minute briefing, many straightening clothing and smoothing down hair. She could feel their eyes on her, and their muted curiosity over the strange woman who had clearly arrived too early.

As she was led into another room—narrower, but much longer than the first reception room—staff carrying trays of champagne were lining up along the walls, beneath a gallery of portraits. At the far end were three tall figures dressed in black, deep in conversation.

Amalie's heart gave a funny jump, then set off at an alarming rate that increased with every step she took towards them. Her escort by her side, she concentrated on keeping her feet moving, one in front of the other.

Suddenly Talos turned his head and met her gaze, his eyes widening with such dumbstruck appreciation that her pulse couldn't help but soar. It was a look men so often threw at her beautiful mother, but never at her. But then, Amalie had never *felt* beautiful before. Tonight, thanks to the hairstylist and beautician Natalia had brought along with her when she'd arrived at the cottage to dress her, she did. She felt like a princess.

And Talos...

Talos looked every inch the Prince.

Like the two men beside him, who matched him in height and colouring, he wore a black tuxedo with a purple bowtie and sash that matched the livery of the palace footmen, and black shoes that gleamed in the same manner as his eyes. For the first time since she'd met him she saw him freshly shaved.

She'd thought the rugged Talos, the man she was getting to know, was as sexy a man as she could ever meet. The princely Talos had lost none of his edge and the wolfish predatory air was still very much there. Not even the expensive dinner jacket could diminish his essential masculinity. He still looked like a man capable of throwing a woman over his huge shoulder and carrying her to a large nomad-style tent to pleasure her in a dozen different ways before she had time to draw breath.

Amalie drew in her own breath as molten heat pooled low inside her at the thought of Talos pleasuring *her*...

Judging from the look in his eyes, something similar was running through his mind.

He strode over to greet her, enveloping her hand in his before leaning down to kiss her on each cheek.

Suddenly she couldn't breathe, her senses completely filled with his scent and the feel of his lips against her skin.

'Little songbird, you are beautiful,' he whispered into her ear, his deep, gravelly voice sending her heart beating so fast it felt as if it would jump out of her chest. 'Let me introduce you to my brothers,' he said while she strove valiantly for composure. 'Helios, Theseus—this is my guest for the evening: Amalie Cartwright.'

Theseus nodded and smiled. 'A pleasure to meet you.'

'And you,' she murmured in reply.

Helios extended his hand to her, his dark eyes studying her. 'I understand you are playing our grandmother's composition at the gala?'

Her cheeks flushing, she nodded and accepted his hand. Suddenly she realised that this was the heir to the throne she was standing before, and bent her knees in a clumsy form of curtsy.

Helios laughed, but not unkindly, before putting his hands on her shoulders and kissing her on each cheek. 'You are my brother's guest—please, do not stand on ceremony.'

'I'm surprised she even tried,' Talos drawled, slipping an arm around her waist and placing a giant hand on her hip.

Dear God, he was *touching* her. Even through

the heavy cloqué material of her dress she could feel the weight of his touch.

'The last time Amalie and I discussed matters of ceremony she reminded me that the French chopped all their royal family's heads off.'

Mortified, she reflexively elbowed him in the stomach, only to elicit more deep laughter from the three Princes that was so contagious her nerves vanished and she found herself laughing along with them.

Although of similar height and colouring, the differences between the brothers were noticeable up close. Theseus, maybe an inch or two shorter than Talos, had a more wiry build and an edgy weariness about him. Helios was as tall as Talos and had a real air of irreverence about him; a man who enjoyed life and was comfortable in his skin.

An officious courtier appeared at their sides and addressed the Princes in Greek.

'We must take our positions,' Talos said quietly.

'Where shall I go?' she asked.

'With me…to greet our guests. Tonight you will stay by my side.'

The gleam in his eyes conveyed a multitude of meanings behind his words. A shivery thrill ran through her, and when he linked his arm through hers she accepted the warmth that followed.

'Where are your brothers' dates?' she asked in a low voice.

'That is the whole purpose of the evening,' he answered enigmatically as they stepped into a cavernous room with a medieval feel, draped with purple sashes. Long dark wood tables formed an enormous horseshoe, laid with gleaming cutlery and crystal glasses that bounced the light from the chandeliers.

She gasped, totally losing track of her interest in his brothers' lack of dates. 'How many people are eating?'

'One hundred and eighty,' Talos answered, grinning.

The Banquet Room never failed to elicit a reaction. And neither, it seemed, did Amalie ever fail to make his senses react. One look and he wanted nothing more than to whisk her away somewhere private and feast on *her*.

With his brothers at the main door, greeting the guests, his role was to welcome them into the Banquet Room and act as host until all the guests had arrived.

Scores of waiting staff were stationing themselves with trays of champagne in hand. Talos helped himself to a glass for them both and passed one to Amalie.

'Drink it in one,' he advised. 'It will relieve the tedium of the next half hour.'

He laughed as she did as he suggested—with enthusiasm and without spilling a single drop.

He could not get over how ravishing she looked. If she hadn't already been there as his guest he would have spent the evening pursuing her, determined to learn everything there was to know about this enchanting stranger in their midst. He would have rearranged the table settings to be seated next to her—would have done everything in his power to keep her as close to him as he could.

But he didn't need to do any of that. For this evening this stunning woman was already his.

'You look amazing,' he said. 'Natalia has outdone herself.'

Strapless, Amalie's gown showed only the slightest hint of cleavage, cinched in at the waist before spreading out and down to her feet, forming a train at the back. It wasn't just the shape of the dress and the way it showcased her slight form that made it so unique, but the heavy material and the colour too—black, with tiny gold sequins threaded throughout into swirling leaves, glimmering under the lights.

The dramatic effect was accentuated by a gold choker around her slender throat, and her dark hair was held in an elegant knot at the base of her neck. She wore large hooped earrings and her eyes were darkly defined, her lips the most ravishing of reds.

Her eyes, wide with obvious awe up until this point, narrowed. 'Has Natalia dressed many of your dates?'

There was a definite hint of tartness in her tone. He eyed her contemplatively. Was that tartness a sign of jealousy?

Jealousy was an emotion he had no time for. He neither cared about his lovers' past bedmates nor felt any pangs of regret when their time was over and they found someone new. If during their time together any sign of possessiveness reared its head, he would end the relationship there and then. Jealousy was dangerous—as dangerous as love itself—driving men and women to lose control of themselves with unimaginable consequences.

And yet hearing that tinge of jealousy filled his chest in a manner he didn't even want to begin contemplating. Not when he couldn't take his eyes from her…couldn't stop his imagination running wild about what lay beneath that stunning dress.

His imagination had run riot since the day before, when she'd played for him semi-naked.

In his head he'd imagined she would wear practical underwear—not the matching lacy black numbers that set off the porcelain of her skin. As slender as he'd imagined, her womanly curves were soft, her breasts high and surprisingly full. What lay beneath those pretty knickers? he'd wondered, over and over. Had she taken the route so many women seemed to favour nowadays? Or had she left herself as nature intended…?

Halfway through her playing he'd smothered a groan, thinking it would be a damn sight better if she were fully naked, as his wild imaginings were utter torture. The expression in her eyes had only added to his torment.

For the first time in his life he'd come close to breaking a promise. He'd known that if he'd taken her into his arms she would have been his. But it hadn't only been his promise that had kept him propped against the cottage wall. It had been the shyness he'd seen when she'd first stood before him wearing only her underwear—a shyness he'd not seen since his lusty teenage years. An innocence that made him certain Amalie had minimal experience with men.

That innocence had acted like an alarm. A warning. Alas, it had done nothing to diminish the ache, which hadn't abated a touch, not in his groin or in his chest. All day, helping his brothers with the evening's arrangements, his mind had been elsewhere—in the cottage, with her.

'Natalia was my grandmother's official dressmaker,' he said softly. 'She made her wedding dress and my mother's wedding dress. She's mostly retired now, but as a favour to me agreed to make your ball gown. I've never sent another woman to her.'

Dark colour stained her cheeks—almost as dark as the wide dilation of her eyes. Was that what her eyes would look like when she was in the throes of passion…?

The thought was broken when the first guests were led into the Banquet Room. Two footmen stood at the door, handing out the evening's booklets—a guide for each guest that was adorned with purple ribbon. Each booklet contained a full guest list, the menu, wine list and a seating plan, along with a list of the music to be played throughout the evening by the Agon Orchestra. The orchestra's role tonight should go some way towards mitigating any underlying resentment that a French orchestra would be playing at the official gala.

As his brothers had already given the official welcome, Talos's job was to keep the guests entertained until everyone had arrived.

He would have preferred to be at the main entrance, shaking hands. He hadn't been joking when he'd described the tedium of what was about to ensue. Almost two hundred guests filed into the Banquet Room, the majority of whom were, at the most, distant acquaintances but all of whom expected to be remembered personally and made to feel like the most important guest there.

Normally Theseus would take this role, and Talos would line up with Helios to do the official greeting. If there was one thing Talos couldn't abide, it was small talk, having to feign interest in interminably dull people. Tonight, though, he wanted to keep Amalie at his side—not wanting her to have to deal with scores of strangers alone. Palace protocol meant only members of the royal family could make the first greeting.

To his surprise, she was a natural at small talk; moving easily between people with Talos by her side, taking an interest in who they were and what they did that wasn't feigned, her smiles as warm for those from the higher echelons of society as for those much further down the social ladder.

If she was aware of all the appreciative gazes being thrown her way by men and women alike she did a good job of pretending not to be.

When the gong rang out, signalling for everyone to take their seats, Talos looked at his watch and saw over half an hour had passed since the first guests had stepped into the Banquet Room. The time had flown by.

'You mastered the room like a pro,' he said in an undertone as they found their seats on what had been designated the top table.

She cast puzzled eyes on him.

'The way you handled our welcome job,' he explained. 'Most people would be overwhelmed when faced with one hundred and eighty people wanting to make small talk.'

She shrugged with a bemused expression. 'My parents were always throwing parties. I think I mastered the art of small talk before I learned how to walk.'

'You attended their parties?'

'I was the main party piece.'

Before he could ask what she meant another gong

sounded out and a courtier bade them all into silence as Helios and Theseus strode regally into the room.

No one took a seat until Helios, the highest-ranked member of the family in attendance, had taken his.

A footman pulled Amalie's chair out for her, while Talos gathered the base of the train of her dress so she could sit down with ease. He caught a glimpse of delicate white ankle and had to resist the urge to run his fingers over it, to feel for himself the texture of her skin.

'Thank you,' she murmured, her eyes sparkling.

'You're welcome.'

Taking his own seat, he opened his booklet to peruse the menu. As Helios had directed, the four-course meal had an international flavour rather than one specifically Greek or Agonite.

White wine was poured into the appropriate glasses, the starter of dressed crab with an accompanying crab timbale, crayfish and prawns was brought out by the army of serving staff, and the banquet began.

'Is your grandfather not attending?' Amalie whispered before taking a sip of her wine.

'He is unwell.'

'Nothing serious, I hope?' she asked with concern.

He forced a smile. 'A touch of flu, that's all.'

'It must be a worry for you,' she said, clearly seeing through his brevity.

'My grandfather is eighty-seven and as tough as a horse,' he deflected artfully.

She laughed. 'My English grandfather is eighty-five and tough as a horse too. They'll outlive the lot of us!'

How he wished that was the case, he thought, his heart turning to lead as he envisaged a life without his grandfather, a steady if often aloof presence, but someone who had always been there.

For the first time he felt the compulsion to confide, to tell the truth of his grandfather's condition. It was there, right on the tip of his tongue. And he was the man who confided in *no one*. Not even his brothers.

The thought was unsettling.

Talos had learned the art of self-containment at the age of seven. The only person able to give him enough comfort to sleep when the nightmares had become too much to bear had died five years ago.

Yet for all the solace his grandmother had given him she'd never been able to give him peace. No one could give him that. He would sit stiffly in her arms, refusing to return the physical comfort she gave him. It had been a battle of wills with himself, something he could control and that no one could ever take away.

He'd been wise not to return the affection. How much greater would his pain have been if he had? He'd loved his mother with the whole of his heart. Her death had come close to destroying him.

The pain of his grandmother's death had still hit him like one of the punches he received in the boxing ring, but it had been survivable. If he'd allowed himself to love her the way he'd loved his mother, he didn't like to think how he would have reacted. Would the control he'd spent most of his lifetime perfecting have snapped? Would he have returned to those awful adolescent days when his fists had lashed out so many times he'd been on the verge of expulsion?

He was saved from having to respond by a young waiter asking if he would like his wine topped up.

If Amalie noticed his changed demeanour she gave no sign of it, craning her neck to follow their wine server's progress out of the room. 'Doesn't that boy work at your gym?'

He was impressed that she'd recognised him. Workout gear was markedly different from the fitted black-and-white waiter's uniform, with the purple ribbon stitched into the sides of the trousers.

'And she's from your gym too,' Amalie whispered, nodding at a young girl in the far corner.

'Most of the kids who work at the gym are working here tonight—it's extra money for them and good experience.'

He had to admit to feeling an inordinate amount of pride, watching them performing their jobs so well. He'd fought the protocol battle a number of years ago, to allow 'his' kids to work at the palace whenever the opportunity arose.

'Do you make a point of employing teenagers?'

'It was one of the reasons I decided to build my own gym—I wanted to employ disaffected teenagers and make them feel a sense of worth in themselves. The kids who work there are free to spar and train whenever they're off duty for no charge.'

'These kids are allowed to *box*?'

'You disapprove?'

'It's one thing for a fully grown adult to choose to get into a boxing ring and have his face battered, but quite another when it's a developing teenager.'

'Teenagers are full of hormones they have to navigate their way through. It's a minefield for many of them.'

'I agree, but...'

'Agon is a wealthy island, but that doesn't mean it's problem-free,' he said, wanting her to understand. 'Our teenagers have the same problems as other Western teenagers. We give jobs and training to the ones living on the edge—the ones in danger of dropping out of society, the ones who, for whatever reason, have a problem controlling their anger. Boxing teaches them to control and channel that anger.'

Hadn't he said something similar to her just the day before, in her cottage? Amalie wondered, thinking hard about the conversation they'd shared. The problem was her own hormones and fear had played such havoc that much of their conversation was blurred in her memory.

'Is that why *you* got into boxing?'

His jaw clenched for the beat of a moment before relaxing. 'I had anger issues. My way of coping with life was using my fists.'

'Was that because of your parents?' she asked carefully, aware she was treading on dangerous ground.

He jerked a nod. 'Things came to a head when I was fourteen and punched my roommate at my English boarding school. I shattered his cheekbone.

I would have been expelled if the Head of Sport hadn't intervened.'

'They wanted to expel you? But you're a *prince*.'

His eyes met hers, a troubled look in them. 'Expulsion was a rare event at my school—who wants to be the one to tell a member of a royal family or the president of a country that their child is to be permanently excluded? But it wasn't a first offence—I'd been fighting my way through school since I was eight. The incident with my roommate was the final straw.'

He couldn't read what was in her eyes, but thought he detected some kind of pity—or was it empathy?

She tilted her head, elongating the swan of her neck. 'How did your Head of Sport get them to change their mind?'

'Mr Sherman said he would personally take me under his wing and asked for three months to prove he could tame my nature.'

'He did that through boxing?' Now she thought about it, Amalie could see the sense in it. Hadn't the kickboxing workouts Talos had forced her into doing created a new equilibrium within her? Already she knew that when she returned to Paris she would join a gym that gave the same classes and carry on with it.

'At my school you had to be sixteen to join the boxing team, but he persuaded them—with the consent of my grandparents—to allow me to join.' He laughed, his face relaxing as he did so. 'Apart from my brothers, I was the biggest boy in the school. There was a lot of power behind my punches, which was what had got me into so much trouble in the first place. Mr Sherman taught me everything we now teach the kids who use our gym—the most important being how to channel and control my anger.'

'Did it work?'

'I haven't thrown a punch in anger since.'

'That is really something.'

Self-awareness nagged at her—an acknowledgement that while Talos had handled his rage through using his fists, she'd retreated from her own fears and buried them. But while he'd confronted and tamed his demons she'd continued hiding away, building a *faux* life for herself that was nothing like her early childhood dreams—those early days when she'd *wanted* to be a virtuoso on the violin, just like her father.

She'd been five years old when she'd watched old

footage of him at Carnegie Hall—the same night he'd played on stage with Talos's grandmother—and she'd said, with all the authority of a small child, 'When I'm growed up I'll play there with you, Papa.'

She'd let those dreams die.

CHAPTER NINE

IT TOOK A FEW beats for Amalie to regain her composure. 'Did you get to take part in proper boxing matches?'

'I was school champion for four years in a row—a record that has never been broken.' He placed a finger to the scar on his eyebrow. 'That was my most serious injury.'

She winced. 'Did you want to take it up professionally?'

'I'm a prince, so it was never an option—royal protocol.' He gave a rueful shake of his head, then flashed another grin that didn't quite meet his eyes. 'I *did* win every amateur heavyweight boxing award going, though, including an international heavyweight title.'

'No!' she gasped. 'Really?'

'It was six years ago.'

'That is incredible.'

'It was the best day of my life,' he admitted. 'Receiving the winner's belt with the Agon National Anthem playing... Yes, the best day of my life.'

She shook her head in awe, a thrill running through her as she saw a vision of Talos, standing in the centre of a boxing ring, perspiration dripping from his magnificent body, the epitome of masculinity...

'Truly, that's incredible. Do you still compete?'

'I haven't boxed in a competitive match since. I knew if I couldn't fight professionally I wanted to retire on a high.'

'You must miss it, though.'

She tried to imagine having to stop playing her violin and felt nothing but coldness. Her earliest concrete memory was receiving her first violin at the age of four. Yes, it had partly been forced on her, but she'd loved it, had adored making the same kind of music as her papa, revelled in her parents' excitement when she'd taken to it with such an affinity that they couldn't resist showing her off to the world. She'd loved pleasing her parents but before she'd reached double digits the resulting attention from the outside world had turned into her personal horror story. She might have inherited her parents' musicality, but their showmanship had skipped a generation.

He shrugged. 'I still spar regularly, but in truth I knew it was time to focus my attention on the business my brothers and I founded. Theseus had gone off on his sabbatical, so Helios was running it almost single-handedly along with dealing with his royal duties. It wasn't fair on him.'

'I don't understand why you all put so much into the business when you have so much wealth.'

He eyed her meditatively. 'How much do you think it costs to run a palace this size? The running costs, the maintenance, the staff?'

'A lot?'

'Yes. A lot. And that's just for one palace. Factor in the rest of our estates—my villa, for example—travelling costs, security...'

'I can imagine,' she cut in, feeling slightly dizzy now he was explaining it.

'My family has always had personal wealth,' Talos explained, 'but a considerable portion of our income came from taxes.'

'Came?'

He nodded. 'My brothers and I were determined to make our family self-sufficient, and three years ago we succeeded. Our islanders no longer pay a cent towards our upkeep. I might not compete any more, but I get all the intellectual stimulation I need.'

Amalie swallowed, guilt replacing the dizziness. She'd been so dismissive of his wealth.

Talos Kalliakis might be unscrupulous at getting his own way but he had a flip side—a side that was loyal, decent and thoughtful. He clearly loved his island and his people.

'What about the physical stimulation you got from competitive boxing?' she asked. 'Have you found a replacement for that?'

His eyes glistened, a lazy smile tugging at his lips. 'There is a physical pastime I partake in regularly that I find *very* stimulating...'

The breath in her lungs rushed out in a whoosh.

When he looked at her like that and spoke in that meaningful tone all her senses seemed to collide, making her tongue-tied, unable to come up with any riposte—witty or otherwise.

For the first time she asked herself why she should. Why make a joke out of something that made her blood and belly feel as warm and thick as melted chocolate? Why continue to deny herself something that could take her places she'd locked away?

Hadn't she punished herself enough?

That thought seemed to come from nowhere, making her blink sharply.

Punished herself enough?

But there was something in that. Her fear was wrapped in so many layers, with her guilt over her role in her parents' divorce bound tightly in the middle of it.

Talos had confronted his fears and mastered them. Wasn't it time she allowed herself the same? She didn't have to suppress her basic biological needs and be a virgin for ever out of fear. Or guilt.

She wasn't her mother. Allowing herself to be with Talos and experience the pleasure she just *knew* she would receive at his willing giant hands wouldn't be a prelude to falling in love. A man holding one hundred musicians' livelihoods to ransom for the sake of a *gala* could pose no risk to her heart.

She cleared her throat and dropped her voice to a murmur. 'Would you care to elucidate on this stimulation you speak of?'

She would swear his eyes darkened to match the melting chocolate in her veins.

He leaned his head forward and spoke into her exposed ear. 'I can do much better than that...'

The chocolate heated and pooled down low, right

in the apex of her thighs…the feeling powerful enough to make her lips part and a silent moan escape her throat.

Just when she was certain he was going to kiss her—or, worse, *she* was going to kiss *him*—activity around them brought her to her senses.

They were in the Banquet Room of the royal palace, surrounded by almost two hundred people, the heir to the throne sitting only six seats to her right. And she was bubbling up with lust.

During the rest of the banquet she made a studious effort to speak to the gentleman on her right, a prince from the UK. Through it all, though, her mind, her senses, her *everything* were consumed by Talos, deep in conversation with the woman to his left, a duchess from Spain.

Somehow their chairs had edged closer so his thigh brushed against hers, and when their dessert of *loukoumades*—a delicious Greek doughnut, drizzled with honey, cinnamon and walnuts—was cleared away, and they were awaiting the final course of fresh fruit, a shock ran through her when his hand came to rest on her thigh.

She wished she'd tried to talk Natalia into a different material for the dress; something lighter. The heavy fabric suited the theatricality of the dress beautifully, but while she could feel the weight of Talos's hand there was none of the heat her body craved.

It wasn't enough.

She wanted to *feel* him.

Sucking in a sharp breath to tame the thundering of her heart, she casually straightened, then moved her hand under the table to rest on his. As she threaded her fingers through his he gave the gentlest of squeezes, and that one simple action sent tiny darts of sensation rippling through her abdomen.

Strong coffee and glasses of port were poured, whilst the British Prince chattered on about one of the charities he was patron of. Amalie tried hard to keep her attention fixed on him, smiling in all the right places, laughing when appropriate, all the while wishing every guest there would magically disappear and leave her alone with Talos.

She hadn't drunk much wine—a couple of glasses at most—but felt as if she'd finished a whole bottle, because at that moment she felt giddily out of control.

Talos still had hold of her thigh, his thumb making circular motions on the material so torturously barricading him from her skin.

She had no idea where her nerve came from—maybe her fingers had a life of their own, because they moved away from his hand to tentatively brush his thigh. He stiffened at her touch, his own hand tightening its hold on her.

The British Prince chattered on, clearly oblivious to the undercurrents playing out beside him.

Slowly her fingers crept over Talos's thigh until her whole hand rested on it. The fabric of his trousers felt silken to her fingers, contrasting with the taut muscularity they covered. She could *feel* him.

He sat as stiff as a statue, making no attempt to move when, with a flush of heat she realised her little finger was right at the crevice of his thigh, the line of the V that connected it to his groin...

A feeling of recklessness overtook her and she swiped the little finger up a little further—deeper into his heat, closer to the source of his masculinity.

The statue came to life.

Talos swept his hand away from her thigh to reach for his port, which he swilled down before putting the glass back on the table. Not that she saw him do any of those things, rather she felt them, her attention still, to anyone interested enough to be watching, fixed on the British Prince.

Then Talos's hand was back under the table and clasping hers, which was slowly stroking his thigh, her little finger brushing the V of his groin. Twisting it so he could hold it tightly, he entwined his fingers in hers.

'Are you okay?' the British Prince asked, pausing in his talk on water sanitation in developing countries. 'You look flushed.'

She felt her neck and cheeks flame. 'I think I need some air, that's all,' she said to the Prince, hoping she didn't sound as flustered as she felt inside.

A warm arm slipped behind her back and round her waist and Talos was there, pressing against her, ostensibly having abandoned his conversation with the Duchess to join in with theirs.

'Don't worry, little songbird,' he said, his deep voice sending reverberating thrills racing through her. 'The banquet will soon be over.'

Talos felt as if he needed air too...

If her hand had moved any higher and actually touched the hardness that was causing him such aching pain he would have come undone on the spot.

Never in his life had he been so aroused, not

even yesterday in the cottage where, despite their lack of clothing, it had been a different arousal.

He sensed no fear in Amalie now.

No, this was a special kind of sweet torture and in front of all Helios's guests he was unable to do a damn thing about it.

So long as he kept her hand away from his crotch he would master it. The most sensible option would be to stop touching her altogether, but sensible didn't count for anything—not when it was Amalie Cartwright he was touching.

He let out a breath of relief when the palace quartet entered the Banquet Room, mandolins and banjos playing out the guests with the folk music beloved of all Agonites.

The Agon royal party rose first. Keeping her hand firmly clasped in his, Talos led Amalie through to the adjoining ballroom, delighting in her gasp of pleasure.

The ballroom was by far the most majestic of all the palace rooms, both in size and stature. With high ceilings and a black-and-white checked floor, even Talos experienced a thrill of stepping into a bygone age whenever he entered it.

As soon as the royal party entered, the orchestra, situated in a corner, began to play.

Most of the guests took seats at the highly deco-
rated round tables lining the walls, free to choose
where they wanted to sit. The two ornate thrones
at the top of the room shone under the swooping
chandeliers. Looking at them sent a pang through
him. They would remain empty for the duration
of the evening.

He wondered how his grandfather was, his stomach twisting at the remembrance of the vomiting
episode he had witnessed just a few short hours
ago. He consoled himself with the knowledge that
should his grandfather take a turn for the worse he
and his brothers would be notified immediately.

Talos guided Amalie to a table and poured them
both a glass of wine. Theseus joined them and, as
was his nature, soon had Amalie giggling as he
regaled her with tales of their childhood.

A strange tightening spread across his chest to
see her so clearly enthralled, and with a start he
realised the cause. Jealousy. *His* jealousy. She'd
never laughed so freely for him.

This was becoming dangerous.

Desire was one thing, but jealousy... That was
one emotion too far and too ugly.

That was what you got for spending so much
time with a beautiful woman without bedding her.

If he'd bedded her from the start her allure would have vanished already and he would now be focussing on getting her performance-fit without wasting energy wondering how she looked naked or whether she moaned loudly when she came.

For all his words about 'partaking' regularly, he hadn't been with a woman in months—not since his grandfather's diagnosis. It was as if his libido had gone into stasis.

And now his libido had gone into hyperdrive.

Forget noble thoughts about not taking advantage of her position on the island, or that she was there because of his blackmail. The chemistry between them had gone off the charts. All they needed was one night to detonate it. One night. Come the morning, their chemistry would be spent. If not, they still had three weeks to expel it completely, but they would have tamed the worst of it. They would be able to concentrate on nothing but her gala performance.

At that moment the orchestra broke into a waltz, indicating the start of the evening's dancing. Talos watched Helios take a deep breath, fix a smile to his face and cross the ballroom to tap a princess from the old Greek royal family on the shoulder. She was on her feet like a shot, allowing him to lead her onto the dance floor. It was the cue for the other guests who fancied trying their hands at traditional ballroom dancing to get to their feet.

'Shouldn't you find a lady to dance with?' Talos pointedly asked his brother in Greek.

Theseus's smile dropped. He grimaced, his eyes darting around the room as if he were searching for someone. 'I'll have a drink first. But don't let me stop you—you two make a beautiful couple.'

Talos narrowed his eyes and fixed Theseus with his 'stare'. Theseus pulled a face and swigged his wine.

'Would you like to dance?' he asked Amalie. Talos might loathe dancing, but the thought of having her in his arms was a temptation not to be resisted.

'I've never waltzed,' she said dubiously.

'Most of our guests have never waltzed. I will lead you.' That was if he could remember. He hadn't waltzed since the Debutantes Ball in Vienna, which his grandfather had forced him to attend when he was twenty-one. If his brothers hadn't already been forced into attendance at the same age he would have put up more than an obligatory protest.

She allowed him to help her to her feet and guide her onto the dance floor.

Facing her, he dropped her hand, took a step back and bowed. 'You must curtsy,' he instructed.

Her luscious lips spread into a smile. 'Certainly, Your Highness.'

He returned the smile and reached for her right hand with his left and held it out to the side. 'Now, place your other hand on my bicep.'

'There's enough of it for me to hold on to,' she answered, that same smile still playing on her lips, her eyes glimmering with a private message to him—a message he understood and that made his blood pressure rise so high his heart felt in danger of thudding out of his ribs.

To hell with the traditional hold, he thought, placing his right hand on her back and resting his fingers on the bare flesh above the lining of the dress.

She felt exquisite.

Soon they were swirling around the room, the enchantment on her face making all the ridiculous ballroom-dancing lessons he and his brothers had been subjected to in their teenage years worthwhile—something he had *never* thought would happen.

Amalie felt as if she'd stepped into heaven. She'd

never waltzed before but it didn't matter; Talos guided her around the dance floor with a tenderness and grace that was as unexpected as it was heavenly.

She had never felt so feminine before either, the security of his arms something she would savour and relish.

The original gap between them when they'd started dancing had closed, and suddenly she was very much aware their bodies were pressed together.

Releasing her grip on his bicep, she smoothed her hand up to clasp the nape of his neck, glad a slower waltz was now being played, one that allowed her time to do nothing but gaze up into his eyes. Her legs followed his lead with no thought.

The heels she wore elevated her enough that her breasts pressed against his chest, his abdomen against the base of her stomach, but to her intense frustration she couldn't *feel* him anywhere other than on her back, where his hand rested, his heat scorching her skin in the most wonderful way imaginable.

'Your brothers seem nice,' she said, frantic to cut through the tension between them before she was forced into something drastic—like dragging him away.

'They're good men,' he agreed, his gaze not dropping from hers.

'What did you mean earlier, when I asked if they had dates and you said that was the whole purpose of the evening?'

He laughed lightly. 'It is time for Helios to end his bachelor days. He is hoping that tonight he will meet someone suitable.'

'Someone suitable? For marriage?'

'Yes. A woman of royal blood.'

'That sounds clinical.'

'He is heir to the throne.'

His fingers were making the same circles on her back that he'd made on her thigh, but this time she could actually feel it. And it felt wonderful.

'It is traditional for the heir to marry a woman of royal descent.'

'Is there a reason why he's looking for a bride now?' She thought of their absent grandfather, the King, and wondered if there was more to his illness than Talos was letting on.

'He's of the right age.'

She felt his muscles ripple as he lifted a shoulder in a shrug.

'He wants to be young enough to enjoy his children.'

'If you marry, will it have to be someone of royal

descent too?' As she asked the question a strange clenching gripped her heart.

'No.'

'So if you marry it will be for love?'

His lips twisted into a mocking grin. 'If I marry it will be because someone has placed a gun to my head.'

'Marriage is a piece of paper. It doesn't mean anything.'

Love was the state she'd always feared—not a commitment so easily broken it wasn't worth the paper it was signed on. It was passionate love that made fools of people. A piece of paper could dissolve a marriage into nothing, but a severed heart never fully healed.

'It means a lot if you're a member of the Kalliakis royal family. Divorce is forbidden.'

That's fine, she thought. *I don't want to marry you. All I want is to touch you. Everywhere.*

That was why she would be safe from the threat of a severed heart. Her passion for Talos was purely physical. When she returned to Paris her heart wouldn't feel a thing, would only skip at memories of being with him.

'Is divorce forbidden for everyone on your island?'

'Only members of the royal family,' he murmured.

'And are you allowed lovers? Before you marry?' she added, dropping her voice even lower.

His eyes were a blaze of molten lava, his strong nose flaring, his jaw clenched. 'If I want a lover no decree is going to stop me.'

Nothing and no one could stop this man doing *anything* he wanted.

The thought should appal her, but it didn't—not when the thought of allowing him to do whatever he wanted was so strong she dug her nails into his neck to stop her fingers yanking at her dress so she could press her bare skin to him. Her desperation to feel him was matched only by her desperation for him to feel *her*.

A finger tapped her shoulder. It was the British Prince. 'May I have the next dance?'

'No,' Talos growled, not looking at him, but tightening his hold on her back and his grip on her hand.

'You can't blame a chap for trying,' the Prince said, laughing ruefully before striding off to find another dance partner.

Talos stopped dancing. The clenching of his jaw

was even more pronounced. 'I have an apartment here in the palace.'

She didn't miss a beat or fake coyness. 'Is it far?'

'It's closer than my villa or your cottage.'

A spark passed between them, so real and powerful she felt it in every atom of her being.

He brought her hand to his lips. 'Follow me,' he murmured.

CHAPTER TEN

HER HAND CLASPED tightly in his, Amalie followed Talos's lead, weaving through the waltzing couples, yearning to run but keeping her pace steady, avoiding eye contact lest anyone wanted to talk.

She could see the door he was leading her to, in the left-hand corner of the great room. The closer they got, the longer his strides became, until they were nodding at the footmen posted there and then slipping out into a corridor she didn't recognise. Judging by the strong scent of food, she figured they had to be close to the palace kitchens.

They took a left into another long corridor, then another and another. Staff were everywhere, all bowing as they passed.

It wasn't until they reached a fifth corridor, this one dimly lit, that they were completely alone.

Talos had her pinned to the wall so quickly there was no chance to draw breath.

His hands clasped her cheeks and his mouth crashed onto hers with a passion her starving body responded to immediately. His tongue swept across her lips, forcing them to part, then darted into her mouth, his resulting groan stoking the heat consuming her.

She responded with fire, cradling his head, returning the kiss with all the hunger that burned inside her for him.

No sooner had it started than he broke the kiss, keeping her pinned to the wall with his strength, his thumbs running in swirls over her cheeks, his brown eyes dark with intensity.

'I have never been closer to ripping a woman's dress off and taking her in public than I was in that ballroom,' he said roughly.

A pulse ran through her, deliciously powerful. In answer, she nuzzled into his hand and kissed his palm.

He stepped back, trailing his fingers down her neck to the edge of her dress, his breathing heavy. 'We're almost at my apartment.'

They set off again to the end of the corridor, walking at a speed only a tiny rate below a run, until they came to a spiralling marble staircase with a heavy rope barrier across the base of it. Talos moved it swiftly, indicating for her to go up. At the top was a small passage with a door at the end and a small security box by the side. He punched in the code and the door swung open.

Lights came on with the motion and Amalie found herself in an enormous masculine living space, richly furnished with plump charcoal-coloured sofas against a backdrop of muted blues and creams. The room's walls were covered in huge colourful paintings.

There was no time for looking with depth. Talos threw his jacket, sash and bow tie on the floor and guided her through the living area and into a bedroom dominated by the largest bed she'd ever seen—an enormous sleigh bed with intricate carvings.

On the wall opposite the door stood a floor-length mirror, edged with the same intricately carved wood. Catching sight of her reflection, she came to a stop.

Was that woman staring back at her with the flushed cheeks and wild eyes really her? Amalie? The woman who had formed a cosy life for herself while shying away from everything this man—this gorgeous man—was offering her? The man staring at her with a hunger she had only ever seen in films.

Transfixed, she watched as he stepped behind

her, not touching her other than to place his hands on the tops of her arms. A small moan escaped her throat when he dropped a kiss in the arch of her neck.

Swaying lightly, she let her eyes flutter closed and sighed as his fingers swept across her shoulder blades and down her spine to rest at the top her dress.

Bending his head to kiss her ear and brush his lips lightly against her temple, he found and unfastened the hidden hook, then pinched the concealed zipper and slowly pulled it down, all the way to the base of her spine. His hands slid back up the exposed flesh to the top of the dress, then skimmed it assuredly down to her hips, exposing her bare breasts. When he released his hold on it the dress fell in a lazy whoosh to her feet, leaving her naked bar skimpy black knickers and gold shoes.

He wrapped an arm around her middle and held her against him, so she could lift her feet one at a time and step out of the vast amount of material. Talos kicked the dress away, then met her eyes in the reflection of the mirror, a dangerous, lustful glimmer in his stare.

Her chest thrust forward, almost begging for his touch.

The hand holding her so protectively brushed over her stomach and up her side, circling round her breasts to trace along her collarbone and up her neck to the base of her head. Slowly he worked at the elegant knot of her hair until he freed it, gently pulling it down to sprawl across her shoulders.

'Have you had many lovers, little songbird?' he asked, inhaling the scent of her hair.

Speech had deserted her; all she was capable of doing was shaking her head.

'Have you had *any* lovers?'

The second shake of her head had more force behind it, but inside she reeled.

Was her virginity *that* obvious?

He must have read the question in her expression. 'I am an expert at reading between lines,' he said enigmatically, before twisting her round to face him. He ran his thumb over her bottom lip. 'Why don't we even things up and you undress me?'

With hands that trembled, she reached for the top button of his shirt, fumbled with it, then found some dexterity and undid it, then the next. Working quickly, aware of the heaviness of his breathing, she undid them all, then spread the shirt open. Not even conscious of what she was about to do, she pressed her lips to his chest and breathed him in, inhaling the muskiness that evoked thoughts of dark forests and adrenaline-filled danger.

His chest rose and swelled, his hand reaching into her hair and gathering it in his fingers.

Her fingers trailed down the thickening black hair to his abdomen and found the hook fastening his hand-stitched trousers. She swallowed as the palm of her hand felt the heat beneath. She unhooked it, but then her nerve deserted her. Suddenly a burst of sanity crashed through the lustful haze she'd been entranced in.

She'd never touched a man intimately before.

She wanted to touch Talos with a need bordering on desperation, but for the first time her virginity was something she was wholly aware of.

How could she be anything but a disappointment to him? A man as rampantly masculine as Talos would have had scores of lovers, all confident in their bodies and sexuality.

Talos felt Amalie's hesitation, felt the fear creep through her.

His suspicions about her being a virgin had been right. He would have been more surprised to learn she'd had *any* lovers.

He didn't care about her reasons for never having had a lover; cared only that at this moment she was here, with him, and that the crazy chemistry between them could be acted upon. Amalie wasn't on the hunt for a relationship any more than he was; her comment about marriage only being a piece of paper had concurred with his own thoughts entirely.

But confirmation of her virginity *did* force him to take a deep breath and try to cool his ardour. All prior thoughts of simply discarding their clothes and falling into bed were gone. He needed to take it slow. He didn't want to hurt her. By the time he made her his he wanted her so turned on but also relaxed, he could enter her without causing any pain.

Gently he twisted her back to face the mirror, placing an arm around her belly. Her eyes closed and her head rolled back to rest on his shoulder, her breath coming in tiny hitches. He could feel her heartbeat hammering with an identical rhythm to his own.

Moving quickly, he unzipped his trousers with his free hand and worked them off, deliberately keeping his boxers on so the temptation to plunge himself straight into her could be more easily denied.

Done, he pressed himself into the small of her

back, felt her tremble, saw her lips part in a silent moan.

'Open your eyes,' he commanded quietly into her ear.

They fluttered open and met his gaze in the reflection of the mirror.

His fingers played on the lace of her knickers and then tugged them down, delighting to find the dark silky hair below. He dipped a finger into her heat and groaned when he found her moist and swollen.

Keeping the pressure there light and rhythmical, he splayed his other hand upwards and captured a raised breast. It fitted perfectly into his hand. He could hardly wait to taste it, to taste every part of her but before he could take her into his arms and carry her to his bed her back arched, her groin pressed hard against his finger and she stiffened. He watched in awe at their reflection. Her eyes were tightly closed, her lips parted, her cheeks flushed. Then she shuddered and became limp in his arms. If she hadn't been secure against him, he had no doubt she would have fallen to the floor.

He'd never seen or felt anything like it—such a primal, animalistic response. It filled him with something he couldn't name...could only feel, gripping his chest.

Keeping her pressed tight against him, he turned her enough to lift her into his arms.

There was no resistance; her eyes gazed into his, dazed bewilderment ringing out. When she reached a hand to press a palm to his cheek he swallowed, his heart beating so fast it had become a painful thrum.

He laid her down on the bed and shrugged his open shirt off, discarding it on the floor.

She'd covered her breasts. He took hold of her hands and carefully parted them, exposing her full nakedness to him.

To his eyes, Amalie was perfect—her arms and legs toned and smooth, her skin soft, her breasts high, ripe peaches, begging to be tasted.

Bringing his head down to hers, he captured her lips. She returned his kiss with passion, her tongue sweeping into his mouth, her hot, sweet breath flowing into his senses. Her hands reached for his head and razed through his hair.

As he deepened the kiss he stroked his fingers down her body, exploring the soft skin, delighting in the mews escaping her throat.

Breaking the kiss, he ran his lips down her

throat and lower, to her breasts, capturing one in his mouth...

Theos.

For the first time since his teenage years he was on the verge of losing control already. He had never felt so constricted by his boxer shorts, the tight cotton material as tight a barrier as steel.

But she tasted so *good*, of a sweet, feminine essence his senses reacted to. Not just his senses. Every part of him reacted to it.

'Is something wrong?' she whispered, uncertainty in her voice.

'No,' he promised, dragging his mouth back up to her lips and kissing her again. 'Everything is perfect.'

Her hands grabbed at his face, her fingers kneading his cheeks before sweeping over his neck and chest and down to his abdomen. This time she didn't hesitate, pushing under the cotton to lightly touch the head of his erection.

Her kisses stopped and she sucked in a breath.

'It doesn't bite,' he teased, smoothing her hair off her forehead.

Her lips twitched into a shy smile and she burrowed her face into his neck before her tongue darted out to lick his skin. She rubbed her leg against him, all the while slowly trailing her fingers down his length, which throbbed madly under her gentle ministrations. She made no attempt to take hold of it, seemingly content simply to stroke and explore. That this only made him harder than ever—something he had not thought possible—only added to his painful ardour. If he didn't find some release soon he feared he might actually combust.

'I don't use birth control,' she whispered into his neck.

'I didn't think you did,' he assured her, moving her hand away so he could lean over to his bedside table, where he dimly remembered throwing a packet of condoms into a drawer. They were still there. He pulled one out and ripped the foil off, all the time keeping his focus on Amalie, who had sat up and was now exploring his chest with her fingers, the expression on her face something close to rapture.

Kissing her first, he got off the bed and tugged his boxers down.

She met his eyes and swallowed.

'Don't be scared,' he murmured, kneeling back on the bed and gently pushing her flat, so her head rested on the pillow and she was laid out beneath him.

Her smile was dazzling. 'I'm not.'

He kissed her again, then disentangled her arms, which had hooked around his neck at the first press of his lips.

Working swiftly, he securely rolled the condom on, then knelt between her parted thighs. He brushed his hands over her beautiful downy hair, a thrill racing through him to feel her damp heat all over again, his arousal increasing when she bucked upwards to meet his touch.

Then, moving slowly, he laid himself on top of her, taking care not to put his full weight on her. Moving even slower, he guided his erection to the welcome warmth of her opening.

Her hands gripped his shoulders, her nails digging into his flesh.

Her eyes were screwed tight shut.

'Look at me, little songbird,' he said, stroking her cheek.

She opened her eyes. That dazed look had returned to them.

He pushed forward a little more, clenching his teeth as he stopped himself from driving in any deeper. Amalie had never done this before. If he were to do what he so desperately wanted and simply plunge deep inside her he would hurt her, no matter how hot and wet she was for him.

Theos, she felt so *tight*.

He inched forward some more, giving her time to adjust before pressing a little further. Each new push forward elicited the same gasp from her lips: a hitch of surprised pleasure.

As he continued to inch slowly into her he brushed his lips against hers, relishing the short, ragged breaths she breathed back into him.

When he was fully sheathed inside her he paused to catch his own breath and closed his eyes, forcing his mind to think of something—*anything*—other than what they were doing at that moment.

But no matter how hard he tried, even with his eyes firmly shut, all he could see was Amalie.

She shifted slightly beneath him, her hands moving from his shoulders to trail down his back, causing thrills of shivers racing down his spine.

Only when he was sure he had control of himself did he withdraw—not all the way, but enough so that when he pushed back he had to grit his teeth more to retain his control.

This was *torture*. The most divine torture he had ever known.

For the first time in his life he truly wished he could make love without the barrier of a condom, to experience every single aspect of it.

He withdrew a little further, pressed back a little deeper.

Once he was certain Amalie had adjusted to this whole new experience, and that there was no discomfort for her, he allowed himself to settle into a rhythm, all the while telling himself to be gentle, to make this special for her.

He'd never experienced anything like it. Every thrust felt as if he were diving deeper into some unknown abyss, one filled with beautiful, dream-evoking colour.

There was something so *pure* about her responses. Nothing was for effect; everything—all her touches, all her kisses, all her soft moans—was an expression of how she was feeling at that moment and the pleasure she was taking from their lovemaking.

When he gripped her bottom and raised it, just enough to let him penetrate a little deeper, her cry into his mouth was the most beautiful sound he'd ever heard. Even though he was desperate for his own relief he held on, keeping the rhythm that had her tossing her head from left to right and made her breath shallow. Then he felt her thicken around him, felt her pulsing at the same moment she breathed out his name and clung to him, burying her face in his neck as her orgasm made her whole body vibrate and shudder.

He held on, waiting until her climax was spent, then raised himself onto his knees and spread her thighs further apart. He wanted to look at her, to drown in those emerald eyes. Placing one hand on her shoulder and the other on her breasts, he upped the tempo, thrusting in and out, gazing at her beautiful face, her wide eyes, her red-kissed lips, revelling in the little pulses that still came from within her, until he took one final, long thrust and his world exploded in colour.

When the jolts racketing through him finally abated his face was buried in Amalie's hair, which was sprawled over the pillow like a fan. Her arms were locked tightly round him; the only sound was the heavy thudding beat of their hearts.

Lethargy spread through him and he eased himself off her, something dim in the back of his sluggish mind reminding him he had the condom to dispose of. Dragging himself off the bed, he could feel her eyes on him as he padded to the bathroom.

He returned a few moments later, his chest tightening to see she'd slipped under the silk sheets. A shy smile played on her lips.

He hadn't thought this through. As a rule, he didn't bring women to his palace apartment, preferring to conduct his affairs in the privacy of his villa, or wherever in the world he happened to be.

It suddenly dawned on him that not only had he broken his unwritten rule of not conducting an affair within the palace walls, but he'd also run from Helios's ball. It was inconceivable that his absence would go unnoticed.

He couldn't bring himself to care. His grandfather was in bed and his brothers would understand. They'd both had their heads turned by beautiful women over the years. The ball was for Helios, and to a lesser extent for Theseus—not for him. He would never need to marry. The burden of continuing the Kalliakis dynasty was in his brothers' hands.

Now that the flush of lust had been satisfied he should get dressed, get a chauffeur to take Amalie back to the cottage. Except…

She stretched under the covers, that smile still playing on her lips. 'Can we do that again?'

Amalie pulled Talos's shirt, discarded on the floor the evening before, closer around her, catching a wonderful whiff of his woody scent. She sighed dreamily.

That had to count as the most wonderful night of her life.

It amazed her to think she'd spent so long denying this sensual side of herself, marvelled that it had ever scared her. What had she been so frightened of? How could such pleasure be terrifying?

She gazed at Talos sleeping, from her vantage point of the bay window, where she'd settled herself earlier. She'd woken with the sun, the buzz in her blood from their passionate night still alive in her veins, zinging too loudly for her to fall back into sleep. Usually she did everything she could to eke out as much sleep as she could muster. But not today.

The view from his bedroom window was stunning, overlooking the palace maze. In the distance lay the open-air theatre the gala was to be held in—an enormous round dome, cut into the ground like something from Middle Earth. Judging by the view, and the fact that if she craned her neck she could see turrets in the distance, she figured his apartment must be in the far left tower of the palace.

The view from the window was nothing compared to the vision on the bed, curled on his side, one arm splayed out where she had been sleeping, as if he'd been seeking her. She wanted nothing more than to crawl back under the covers, but was determined to hold back and let him sleep. After all their lovemaking he would be exhausted.

She smiled. In sleep he looked curiously vulnerable.

For the first time in her life she felt complete. Like a woman. Like she'd discovered a glorious secret. And at that moment she was happy to savour it and hold it close.

Talos stirred, his hand groping. He lifted his head.

'Bonjour,' she said softly, resting her chin on her knee.

He stretched onto his back and smiled lazily. *'Kalimera,* little songbird. Did you sleep well?'

She gave him a coy smile. 'No.'

'You should come back to bed, then.'

'I should,' she agreed, adopting the same mock serious tone.

He threw the sheets off him, unabashedly displaying his large erection.

Moisture filled her mouth and pooled down low. Sliding off the ledge of the bay window, she padded over to the bed. No sooner had she climbed on than Talos's huge hands were at her waist, pulling her over to straddle him.

He stared into her eyes, trailing a hand down the valley between her breasts. 'No regrets?'

She shook her head and sighed as his fingers found her nipple. 'No regrets.'

'Then make love to me, you sexy woman, and prove it.'

Sexy? *Her?* Sexy was a word she'd never associated with herself before.

Yet as she sheathed him, then sank down onto him, taking the whole of him inside her, she realised she'd never felt as sexy and as alive in her life.

And, dear heaven, it felt amazing.

CHAPTER ELEVEN

WAS IT TRULY possible to become addicted to sex?

The question played happily in Amalie's mind as she sat beside Talos in his Maserati, making polite noises as he pointed out a pile of stones he assured her had once been a monastery. Because there was no doubt about it—she was in lust. Glorious, incredible, beautifully reciprocated *desire*. It was basic biology at its finest. And it didn't frighten her in the slightest.

He'd taken her out for lunch in Resina, the main town on the island, and now they were driving back to her cottage, taking the scenic route through Agon's verdant mountains, avoiding wandering sheep and goats who seemingly had no sense of the danger posed by moving vehicles.

The view on this blue, cloudless day was spectacular, the Mediterranean was gleaming in the distance, and the temperature was sitting comfortably in the mid-twenties. She was mostly oblivious to it, too busy anticipating the moment they'd return to the privacy of the cottage to concentrate on nothing so mundane as *scenery*.

In the two weeks since the ball they hadn't spent a night apart. They'd returned to her cottage on the Sunday, leaving through Talos's private exit so at least she'd been spared the embarrassment of bumping into his brothers, and had more or less lived there since.

Amalie would work on the score during the day, while he went to his villa or the palace to do his own work. In the evening he would collect her and take her to the gym, then they would return to the cottage and make love, and would often still be awake when the sun came up.

She could now play her violin for him with hardly any nerves at all, although she still didn't feel ready to play his grandmother's piece. She wanted to be note-perfect for that. Her orchestra would arrive on Agon tomorrow morning; her first scheduled rehearsal with them was in the afternoon. They would know then if she had truly made progress.

For today, Talos had insisted on taking her out and showing her Agon, arguing that it was a Saturday and that in the three and a half weeks she'd been on his island she'd hardly seen any of it. She would have been happy to stay at the cottage and make love, but he'd brushed her arguments aside with his usual authority, claiming her lips to whisper, 'We'll only be gone a few hours.'

'What are you thinking about?' he asked now, casting a quick sideways glance at her.

Her gaze drifted to his hands, holding the steering wheel with deft assuredness in much the same manner as he handled her.

'Sex,' she answered, tingles racing through her at the thought of their imminent return to privacy and all the things they would do...

He burst into deep laughter. 'Do you ever think about anything else?'

She pretended to think about it before shaking her head. 'No.'

'I am tempted to ask *exactly* what you're thinking about in connection to sex, but if I crash the car it will take us longer to get back,' he said drily. 'You can tell me in graphic detail exactly what you're thinking later.'

'I will,' she murmured, her eyes drifting to his muscular thighs, barely contained in his chinos.

'Can I ask you a personal question?'

His voice had taken on a serious hue that made her twist on the seat to face him properly. 'What do you want to know?'

'Why did you wait until you were twenty-five before having sex for the first time?'

It was the question she'd been waiting a fortnight for him to ask. She was still no more prepared with an answer.

She pressed her cheek to the back of the seat. If she couldn't touch him she could at least look at him.

'I never set out to stay a virgin, but I avoided relationships where lust and desire were the driving forces—I've seen my mother's heart broken too many times to have any faith in passionate *love*. The flame is too bright and burns to ashes too quickly. I didn't understand it was possible to have a passion for someone that is purely about sex.'

'Is that all this is to you?' he asked, a surprising edge to his voice. 'Sex?'

'Isn't that all it is to *you*?' she asked right back, momentarily confused.

He was quiet for a moment, before laughing. 'You're right—what we are sharing is just sex. I admit I find it disconcerting to hear that coming from a woman, and even more disconcerting to actually believe it.'

'Do all your lovers say it's just sex?'

'I set out the ground rules from the beginning.

I make it clear I only want a physical relationship and they all agree.' He pulled a mocking face. 'It never takes them long to change their minds and think they can be the one to tame me.'

'I don't think anyone could tame you,' she commented idly, and swallowed away the strange acrid taste that had formed in her throat. It was no secret he'd enjoyed numerous lovers before her, and would enjoy more when she returned to Paris in little more than a week. 'You're as tameable as a fully grown wolf with territory problems.'

Now his laughter came in great booming ricochets. 'I enjoy my life. I have no wish to be tamed.'

She eyed him shrewdly, wondering why she didn't quite believe him. She believed his words, but there was a part of Talos he kept closed off. Physically, he was the most generous and giving lover she could have dreamt of, but he had demons inside him she couldn't reach—demons she caught glimpses of when he would shout out in his sleep, cries in Greek she didn't understand.

She'd asked him about it and he'd affected ignorance, saying he didn't remember his dreams. She didn't believe him but hadn't pushed the subject. If he wanted to open up to her, he would. And, really, she was hardly in a position to demand to learn all his secrets when their whole relationship was based on sex and getting her performance-ready for the gala.

'So you've never had a relationship of any kind?' he asked.

'I've had boyfriends,' she corrected him, 'Quite a few of them.'

'And they didn't try to get you into bed? Were they gay?'

She gave a bark of surprised laughter. 'I suppose it's possible, but the relationships weren't like that. It was more about a meeting of minds than physical chemistry.'

'Isn't that what normal friends are for?'

'Probably.' She swallowed. 'We would kiss… But my boyfriends were the type of men who were happier to spend an evening discussing Mozart's eccentricities and how it affected his music rather than trying to get me into bed.'

He flashed her a grin. 'I don't pretend to know anything about Mozart, but if I did I can assure you I would be happy to discuss him with you— provided I could be stripping you naked at the same time.'

'But that's what I was hiding from,' she confessed.

'You liked those men because they made you feel safe?' he asked.

For such a physically imposing man Talos was incredibly perceptive—something she was coming to understand more on a daily basis.

'I…' She stopped to gather her thoughts. 'Yes. You're right. After my parents divorced my mother fell head over heels for so many different men that I lost count, but she couldn't hold on to any of them. Her heart was broken so many times it was painful for me to watch.'

'Why couldn't she hold on to them?'

She shook her head and inhaled deeply. 'I don't know. I *think* it was because my father spoilt her during their marriage. He adored her, you see— worshipped her. He treated her like his queen for fifteen years. It was what she was used to and what she expected. And I think it's what pushed her lovers away—they would fall for her beauty and fame, but as soon as they found the needy woman inside they would run a mile. It hurt her very badly. She would smile and sing to the world, pretend nothing was wrong, but behind closed doors she would wail like a child.'

'And you witnessed this?'

She nodded.

'I can understand why that must have been painful for you,' he said quietly.

Hadn't he witnessed his own mother's pain enough times to know how damaging it could be? Especially to a child? The helplessness of being too small and insignificant to offer any protection—either an emotional or a physical sort.

'I know you must think my mother is a brat, and she *is*. But she's also funny and loving and I adore her,' she added with defiance.

'I can tell,' he said wryly, turning the car into the road marking the start of Kalliakis land. 'But you have to admit that it isn't fair of her to place all her emotional problems on *your* shoulders.'

'She can't help the way she is. And, fair or not, it's no less than I deserve.'

'What do you mean by that?'

She didn't answer, turning her face away from him to look out of the window.

'Amalie?'

She placed a hand to her throat, her words coming out in a whisper. 'Her misery is all my fault. If it wasn't for me, my father would never have divorced her.'

A lump formed in his throat at the raw emotion behind her words. 'I don't believe that for a minute.' How could a child influence its parents' marriage? 'But I am surprised to learn that your father divorced her. From what you've said, I assumed your mother had divorced *him*.'

'My father worshipped the ground she walked on but to protect me from her ego he divorced her when I was twelve.'

The pieces were coming together. 'Which was around the time you were pulled from the spotlight. I assume the two things are connected?'

'Yes,' she admitted hoarsely, before closing her mouth with a snap.

He brought the car to a stop outside her cottage and reached out to stroke the beautiful hair that felt like silk between his fingers. He wanted to gather her in his arms, not just to devour her body but to give her comfort. It was a feeling so alien to him that the lump in his throat solidified.

Giving comfort implied a form of caring, and if there was one thing Talos avoided with the zeal of a medic avoiding the plague it was caring. Sex wasn't meant to be anything but fun; it was an itch to be scratched. Nothing more.

Before he could withdraw she turned her face back to him and raised her hand to palm his cheek. Helpless to resist, he brought his mouth down to hers and breathed her in, his heart thundering as he felt her own inhalation and knew she was breathing *him* in in turn.

Being with her was like living in a fugue of desire—a constant state of arousal that needed no encouragement.

It struck him that touching her and being touched in return was becoming as necessary to him as breathing.

Theos.

He *had* to keep his mind focussed on the bigger picture.

No matter how good the sex was between them it didn't change the fact that Amalie was in Agon for the gala and that it was his job to get her on the stage and performing for his grandfather. She had come on enormously in the past fortnight, but still she wouldn't play his grandmother's composition for him, although she would perform other pieces. She swore she knew it by heart and only wanted to perfect it, and he believed her, but the clock was ticking painfully. The gala was only a week away.

Where had the time gone?

He could sense she was close to unbuttoning the secrets she clutched so tightly, and knew it was the key to unlocking what she kept hidden—the thing at the very centre of her stage fright.

A creamy envelope lay on the welcome mat of the cottage, the sight of which made him blink rapidly. It was an official royal envelope.

Amalie opened it as she walked into the living room. 'I've been invited for dinner with your grandfather,' she said, passing it to him.

His heart accelerating, he read the invitation, which was for dinner that coming Wednesday.

'Did you know about this?' she asked.

'No.'

He hadn't been told a thing. Naturally his grandfather's permission had been sought before Talos began his quest to find a soloist, his only wish concurring with Talos's—that the soloist had to be special. Other than that, his grandfather had been content to leave all the organisation for the gala in his grandsons' capable hands, his energy reserves too limited for him to want any part in it.

Talos shouldn't be surprised that he had sought out Amalie before the gala, and made a mental note to tell his grandfather he would be attending too. Astraeus Kalliakis still grieved the love of his life, and would want to meet the woman chosen to step into her footsteps on the stage.

He knew he should take the opportunity to tell Amalie the truth about his grandfather's condition. Prepare her. But the words stuck in his throat, a cold, clammy feeling spreading through his skin as it always did whenever he thought of what the coming months would bring.

The death of the man who had raised him from the age of seven. The man who had come into Talos's bedroom and woken the small boy from his sleep, had taken him into his arms and told him in a voice filled with despair but also with an underlying strength that Talos's parents wouldn't be coming home. That they were dead—killed in a road crash on their way to an event at the Greek Embassy.

It was the only time his grandfather had ever held him in such an informal manner. He'd then left Talos in the care of his Queen, Talos's grandmother, and flown to England so he could personally tell his two other grandsons at their boarding school.

Talos thought back to how it must have been for his grandfather, having to break such tragic news while grieving the loss of his own child. His quiet strength had been something for Talos to lean on in those dark few moments when he'd learned his whole world had been turned upside down and inside out. It had been the last time Talos had ever allowed himself to lean on anyone.

And now his grandfather was nearing the end of his own life.

And there wasn't a damn thing Talos could do about it.

He could no more protect his grandfather from death than he'd been able to protect his mother from his father's fists and infidelities.

'Is something wrong?' Amalie asked, peering at him closely. 'You look a little pale.'

He swallowed and returned her stare, suddenly wishing he could throw his arms around her waist and rest his head on those soft breasts, feel her gentle fingers running through his hair, soothing all the pain away.

He wrenched his thoughts from such useless wishes.

To vocalise it...to reveal the truth about his grandfather... *Theos*, he couldn't even speak of it to his brothers. They skirted around it in conversation, none of them prepared to be the one to speak up, as if saying it would make it true.

He ignored her question, reaching out to stroke her cheek, to have one quick touch of that beautifully textured skin before he continued the conversation they'd started in the car. Except Amalie leaned in and hooked her arms around his neck, her breath on his skin as she razed his throat with her mouth before stepping onto her toes to claim his lips.

Her tongue swept into his mouth, her warm breath seeping into his senses. Wrapping his arms around her, he selfishly took the solace of her kisses, the place where all thought could be eradicated in the balm of her mouth and the softness of her willing body.

The last coherent thought to go through his mind as he carried her up the stairs to the bedroom was that he was nothing but putty in her hands.

Amalie stretched luxuriantly, then turned onto her side to run her fingers over Talos's chest, tugging gently at the dark hair that covered it, brushing the brown nipples, pressing her palm down to feel the heavy beat of his heart.

He grabbed her hand and brought it to his mouth, planting a kiss to her knuckles.

She stared into his eyes, those irresistible brown depths, and a feeling of the utmost contentment swept through her. She could stare at him and lie in his arms for ever…

His hand made circular motions in the small of her back. She raised her leg a touch, pressing her pelvis into his thigh. It didn't matter how deep her orgasms were, still she wanted more. And more…

'You're insatiable,' he growled.

'That's your fault for being so sexy,' she protested with a grin, moving her hand lower.

His eyes gleamed, but he grabbed her hand and brought it back up to rest at his chest. '*You*, my little songbird, are the most desirable woman alive.'

My little songbird?

The possessive pronoun made her heart jolt and soar in a motion so powerful it reverberated through her whole body, right down to the tips of her toes.

My little songbird.

And in that moment came a flash of recognition of such clarity that her heart stuttered to a stop before stammering back into throbbing motion.

This wasn't about lust and desire.

She loved him.

Loved him. *Loved him.*

CHAPTER TWELVE

STRUGGLING TO COMPREHEND, Amalie detached herself from his arms and sat up, crossing her legs to stare down at the face she had, without knowing how or when, fallen in love with.

'Is something the matter?' he asked, his eyes crinkling in question. 'You look as if you've seen a ghost.'

She shook her head, partly to refute his question and partly in wonder that this could have happened to her. She waited for self-recrimination to strike, but the wonder of the moment was too great, her mind a jumble.

Shaking her head again, she said, 'You forcing me here…that horrible contract you forced me to sign…the threats you made…'

He winced and she was glad. She *wanted* him to be ashamed of his behaviour. It meant he had a conscience. And if he had a conscience that meant he was the flesh-and-blood man she'd got to know these past few weeks and not the terrifying ogre she'd first met. It meant they had a chance. A small chance, she knew. Tiny. But a chance all the same.

She rubbed her thumb over his bottom lip and said softly, 'Just because I think you're the sexiest man alive, it doesn't mean I've forgotten what you did to get me here and the abhorrent threats you made.'

But did it mean she'd forgiven him? Talos wanted to know. He opened his mouth to ask, but then closed it.

What if she said no? What if she said she could never forgive him for how he'd got her here and the threats he'd made?

Why did he even *want* her forgiveness? He'd never sought forgiveness before.

Recalling the intimidation he'd put her under to get her acquiescence made him feel tight and compressed inside, and his skin felt as if claws were digging into it. Ruthless behaviour when necessary was nothing new to him, but it had a different taste when you had spent the previous night in bed with the recipient of that behaviour. It tasted different when you knew you would maim anyone who would dare even dream of hurting a hair on the head of that person.

It suddenly struck him that he would give his life to protect this woman.

And as the shock of that revelation filtered through him she continued to speak, cross-legged beside him, naked, the sheet twisted on her lap.

'Whatever the initial circumstances, I can't help thinking coming here is the best thing that could ever have happened to me.'

'Why?' His voice sounded distant and his head was spinning, his pulse racing so hard nausea gripped the lining of his stomach.

'Because being here has given me the time and space to see things clearly.' She dipped her head and gnawed at her bottom lip before speaking again. 'One of my psychiatrists told me outright that he thought I didn't want to be fixed. He was wrong. I...' Her voice caught. When she looked at him her eyes were glassy. 'It's not that I didn't want to be fixed...it's that I didn't think I *deserved* to be fixed.'

Talos ran a hand over his jaw, at a loss as to what he could say. She was unbuttoning herself to him, ready to spill her secrets, and all he wanted to do was shout out and beg her to stop.

He didn't want to hear them. He didn't want to

feel anything else for her. Not pity, not empathy. He would take his guilt like a man, but nothing more.

'Maybe you can understand the early part of my life,' she said, oblivious to the turmoil going on within him. 'You've always been public property too. Before I'd reached the age of ten I'd played for the President of France, had taken part in a celebrity-led anti-poverty concert that was beamed around the world to a billion people...'

All of these facts were things he'd learned when he'd first discovered her in that practice room and known she was 'the one'. It had made her refusal to perform at the gala all the more ridiculous to his mind.

'I was a household name, a child prodigy, and it was easy for me.' She shook her head ruefully. 'I loved performing and I loved the applause. But then I turned ten. I found the reviews my parents had kept of my performances and realised that people had *opinions* about my music—that they weren't just enjoying it but dissecting everything about it. They were dissecting *me*. All the joy I'd experienced on stage evaporated.'

She snapped her fingers.

'Gone. I'd never experienced fear once, and all of a sudden I was crippled by it. What if they found me wanting? What if the way I interpreted a particular piece compared unfavourably to another violinist? So many thoughts and fears, when before there had been nothing but the joy of playing. It all came to a head on my mother's birthday, when I was twelve.'

She broke away and reached for the glass of water on the bedside table.

'What happened?' he asked, once she'd placed the glass back. She'd stopped talking, clearly gathering her thoughts together.

'She had a party at our holiday home in Provence. I'd spent two years begging not to play in public any more, begging to go to school and make friends, begging for a normal life—but she wouldn't allow it. I was *special*, you see, and, in my mother's eyes I belonged on the stage, receiving the plaudits she took for granted in her own career.'

Her voice dropped.

'I love my *maman*, but she can be very manipulative. She was not ashamed to use emotional blackmail to get me to play. She'd had a stage built at the bottom of the garden. I remember standing on it and seeing all those eyes upon me—there were at least a hundred guests, most of them international household names—and I froze. And then...'

'And then?'

Her eyes were huge on his. 'I wet myself. In front of all those people. They all saw it. All of them. They stopped talking amongst themselves and stared at me—and, God, the *horror* in their eyes. The humiliation was excruciating.'

Talos's throat had closed completely. He thought back to the clip he'd found on the internet, of her at her last public performance, before she'd retreated from the limelight. It could only have been months before the party she'd described. She'd been a scrap of a girl at twelve, without any of the knowing precociousness of preadolescence, and small for her age. She'd been a *child*.

Amalie sighed and visibly gathered herself together, tucking her hair behind her ears.

'Maman was mortified, but she swore it was just a blip. I was booked to play at the Royal Albert Hall a week later, as part of a Christmas celebration, and she insisted I still play. My father tried to get her to see reason but she couldn't—really, she *couldn't*. I was her protégée; she'd created me. Minutes before I was due to go on stage I had a panic attack, bad enough that a stagehand called an ambulance. When I was released from hospital my father collected me alone. Maman had refused to listen to reason so he felt he had no choice but to leave her and take me with him for my own protection.'

She blew out a long puff of air and gave a laugh that was full of bitterness rather than humour.

'He loved her, but he knew that by staying with her he would be condoning her treatment of me. Since then I've watched my mother rebound from relationship to relationship, knowing that if I'd been stronger they would still be together—'

'No,' he cut in, finally finding his voice. 'No, it was your mother—not you. You were a child.'

Her eyes caught his and she jerked her head in a nod, relief spreading over her features that he understood.

'That's what I mean about it being good for me here in Agon,' she said. 'It's given me the space and perspective to see reason and the time to think. You see, even though my father was awarded custody of me, given sole responsibility for my welfare, I still spent holidays and weekends with her. He never stopped me seeing her. He never stopped loving her but he felt he had to put my well-being first and take any decisions about my welfare out of her hands. I watched them both suffer apart and all I could see was that it was *my* fault. I felt as if I'd destroyed their lives. I've been punishing myself because subconsciously I didn't think

I deserved to have the future I'd dreamed about. I created a nice, safe life for myself and thought it was enough.'

'And now?' he asked. 'You've come so far already. You've played for me, which in itself was a huge hurdle to overcome. Your orchestra will be here tomorrow, so we will see how successful we have been, but I have faith. You can do this, my little songbird. But you need to want this for yourself, regardless of any repercussions.'

Her head tilted. 'Do those repercussions still exist?'

'I don't know,' he said honestly. 'I would prefer not to find out.'

'So would I.' A sad smile spread over her face. 'It is hard for me to reconcile the man I'm sharing a bed with with the brute who forced his way into my home.'

'They're one and the same. I make no apologies for being the man I was raised to be. When it comes to my family and my country I fight—and when necessary I fight dirty.'

'That you certainly do,' she said with a sigh, before reaching for his hand and threading her fingers through his. 'Why is this gala so important to you? I understand a nation's pride in half a century of successful and prosperous rule by one monarch, but I can't help thinking it means more to you than that.'

'You don't think that's enough?' he deflected. 'Fifty years of rule is no easy feat. In Agon most monarchs abdicate when their heir reaches forty, allowing them to enjoy their retirement. My grandfather's heir died before he reached that age, so he was left with no choice but to carry on—which he has done with dignity and pride, for his people. Helios will be forty in four years.'

Before she could ask another question he pulled her down to him and rolled her onto her back. Devouring her mouth, he allowed the sweetness of her touch, the sweetness of *her*, to encompass him and drive away the tightness pinching his skin to his bones.

And as he moved in her, her soft moans dancing in his ear and the short nails of her left hand scratching and gripping his back and buttocks with as much need as the long nails of her right, his mind emptied of everything but the ecstasy he experienced in her arms.

Talos had dozed off. Amalie lightly traced the bow of his full top lip, resisting the urge to replace her finger with her mouth. He looked at peace, all that latent energy in hibernation.

She'd told him everything. About all the shame she carried, the shame she hadn't even known she was carrying—not just what had occurred at her mother's birthday party but the knock-on effects. Talking about it, admitting it—not just to Talos but to herself—she'd felt cleansed. Purged. He was right. She'd been a child.

Her heart felt so full, and it was all because of him. He'd stolen her heart and it astounded her how willing she'd been in allowing him to take it. But then he'd marked her with that first look. She'd stood no chance, not once she was on his island. Not once he'd shown her his human face. Even that damnable contract didn't make her fists clench any longer. She loved that he was prepared to fight for what he believed in.

What would it be like, she thought wistfully, to have this great man's love? To be enveloped under the protection he extended to his family and his people?

She couldn't allow herself to think like that. She was not her mother. Accepting that she'd fallen in love with him did not give her any illusions that he would have fallen for her in return. Only a few hours ago he'd made it clear it was all about sex.

But hadn't she said exactly the same thing? And hadn't she meant it too?

No. She would not allow herself the futility of hope. While she was on Agon she would cherish the time she spent with him. When it was time for her to leave she would go with her head held high and slip back into her old life.

She blinked.

Did she even *want* to go back to her nice, cosy existence?

Prickles spread out over her skin as she thought about what the future could hold for her. The future she'd once dreamt about.

She'd been terrified of passion and love. With Talos she had found both and she was still standing. Not only standing, but with an energy fizzing in her veins that made her feel more alive than she'd ever known.

All the walls she'd built—in part to protect herself, in part to punish herself—had been dismantled, revealing a future that could be hers if only she had the courage to reach out and take it.

Talos was a fighter. He wore his courage in his skin. He'd forced her to fight too, had found a way to bring out her own inner warrior. Now she needed to hold that inner warrior close and never let it go.

Slipping out of the covers, she helped herself to his discarded black T-shirt and tugged it over her head as she made her way down the stairs and into the living room. There, she opened her case, tightened and slid resin over her bow, tuned her violin. Then she took one final deep breath and went back up to the bedroom.

Talos still slept, but he'd shifted position in the few minutes she'd been gone. The moment she sat on the edge of the bed he opened his eyes.

Heart thundering, she smiled shyly at him, then closed her eyes, tucked her violin under her chin and positioned the bow.

The first note rang out with a high sweetness that hit Talos like a punch in his gut, waking him fully in an instant.

She didn't need to tell him. He knew.

This was his grandmother's piece. Her final composition, never before played to a living soul.

And as he listened, watched Amalie play, the punches continued to rain down on him, throwing him back a quarter of a century to his childhood, to the time when his whole world had been ripped apart.

Whereas before he'd been eager to hear her play it, now he wanted to wrestle the violin from her hands and smash it out of the window. But he was powerless to move, to stop the music from ringing around the bedroom, to stop the memories from flooding him. He was as powerless as he'd been when he was seven years old, unable to stop his father throwing blows upon his mother.

As he was assailed by all those torrid memories something else stole through him—a balm that slowly crept through his veins to soothe his turmoil, forcing the memories from his mind and filling him with nothing but the sweet music pouring from Amalie's delicate fingers.

It was like listening to a loving ghost. If he closed his stinging eyes he could see his grandmother. But she wasn't there. It was Amalie, who had interpreted the music with love and sympathy and such raw emotion it was as if Rhea Kalliakis had pointed a finger down at her from heaven and said, *She's the one.*

To watch her play felt like a precious gift in itself—a gift to love and cherish for ever.

It wasn't until she played the final note that she

opened her eyes. He read the apprehension in them, but saw something else there too—an emotion so powerful his heart seemed to explode under the weight of it.

He dragged a hand down his face and inhaled through his nostrils, trying to restore an equilibrium that was now so disjointed he couldn't find the markers to right it.

'When my parents died I suffered from terrible nightmares.' His words were hoarse from the dryness in his throat. 'My grandmother would sit on my bed, as you are now, and she would play for me until the nightmares had gone and I had fallen back to sleep.'

Amalie didn't answer; her eyes wide and brimming with emotion.

'You've brought her music to life,' he said simply.

She hugged her violin to her chest. 'It's the most beautiful piece of music I've ever been privileged enough to play, and I promise you I will fight as if I were Agon-born to play it at your grandfather's gala.'

His heart twisted to see the fierceness on her face. He knew it was directed at herself, knew the battle wasn't yet won, but also that she would fight with everything she had to overcome half a lifetime of fear. There was something about the way she looked at him that made him think she wouldn't be fighting solely for the sake of the contract and the repercussions that would come from failure, but for *him*.

And the thought of her fighting for him made his disjointed equilibrium do a full spinning rotation.

CHAPTER THIRTEEN

TALOS GOT INTO his car and turned on the ignition. He'd barely cleared his villa before he turned the car back and turned the engine off.

He imagined her cottage, in the distance, hidden from where he sat by dense trees. He imagined her waiting by the door for him, dressed in the tight-fitting sweats that showed off her slender curves. Imagined the welcoming kiss she would give him, her enthusiasm, as if they'd been parted for weeks rather than a few hours.

Since she'd played for him in the bedroom she'd had no problem with him being around while she practised his grandmother's piece. The problem was that her orchestra had arrived a couple of days ago and proper rehearsals for the gala had begun. Amalie had taken to the stage for the first rehearsal and frozen.

Today he'd been there to witness it for himself—and this time she'd played it to the end, but only by keeping her terror-filled eyes on him. She'd visibly trembled throughout, and the notes she'd played had been tense and short—nothing like the flowing, dreamlike melody she achieved when they were alone.

Her obvious distress felt like sharpened barbs in his heart.

It was too soon for her. Maybe if the gala were in a couple of months, or even weeks, there would be time but it was only four days away. She knew her part perfectly, and the orchestra knew theirs, but what use was that when she couldn't get her fingers to work?

And he, arrogant bastard that he was, had forced this nightmare on her, believing that some fighting spirit could cure half a lifetime of severe stage fright.

There was no way to fix it in time, not without putting her through an enormous amount of distress.

Tomorrow she would dine with his grandfather. Talos had invited himself along as well and hadn't liked the look in his grandfather's eyes when he'd suggested he come. It had been far too knowing.

Amalie's solo was the one performance of the whole gala that his grandfather was looking forward to. He might have to miss large chunks of the ceremony, but he had told Talos only yesterday that he would sooner be in his coffin than miss her performance.

Swallowing the acrid bile in his throat, Talos dug his phone out of his pocket and called her. 'I'm going to have to give tonight a miss,' he said, speaking quickly. 'Something's come up.'

'Are you all right?' The concern in her voice was plain.

He didn't want her concern. He didn't deserve it. The only thing he deserved was a dozen punches to his gut for forcing this nightmare on her.

'I'm busy with work, that's all. I'll try and catch up with you later.'

He blew out a breath of stale air as he disconnected his phone and tried to clamp down on the emotions raging through him, the feeling that his whole life was converging in a tipping point over which he had no control.

Amalie stepped through the trees surrounding her cottage and gazed at the villa in the distance. The moonless night was dark, but the white building glowed brilliantly under the stars.

It took her ten minutes to cross the land and reach it, and by the time she knocked on the front door her heart was thundering at a rate of knots, her hands clammy. She'd never been inside Talos's villa before. It occurred to her that she'd never been invited. His villa was very much his private sanctuary. Kept apart from her.

All evening she'd been waiting for another call from him or a knock on the cottage door. Something was wrong, and had been for the past couple of days. There was an unbreachable distance between them.

She knew he was worried about the gala. She was too. Terrified about it. They'd both had such confidence that she was ready to play in public, but that confidence had been a deception. Her nerves were winning the war. She'd just about managed to scrape through the rehearsal earlier, when she'd had his face to focus on, but her shaking fingers had prevented any hint of musicality.

Was that the reason for his distance?

Frustration and disappointment with her?

The maid who opened the door recognised her and welcomed her in with a smile. As neither spoke the other's language, the maid beckoned Amalie to follow her.

The interior of the villa was as fresh and modern as the palace was old and medieval, but with a definite nod to Agon's Minoan ancestry; Greek sculptures and artwork adorned the walls.

After leading her down a wide flight of marble stairs and through a large door the maid stopped and pointed at another closed door, gave a quick bow, and disappeared back up the stairs, leaving Amalie on her own.

Heart in her mouth, she tapped on the door. When there was no answer she rapped again, louder, pressing her ear to it. She heard nothing. She chewed her lips before deciding to turn the handle. She pushed the door ajar and peered through the crack, pushing it wide open when she realised this was Talos's personal gym.

Weight-lifting equipment, a treadmill and a rowing machine—items she wouldn't have known one from the other a month ago—were lined up against the mirrored wall opposite the doorway. Through the same mirror she caught sight of a blur and turned to the left.

There he was, oblivious to her presence, thrashing the living daylights out of a punching bag.

She knew she should call out to him, let him know she was there, but she was captivated by what she saw.

All he wore was a pair of black shorts. His feet

were bare, his hands gloveless. She winced to imagine the damage he could be doing to his fingers, her chest constricting as she realised something must be seriously wrong for him to forgo the gloves he always insisted on. Only the week before she'd seen him admonish a teenager for daring to hit a basic pad without gloves. A punching bag was a much harder target.

All the same, she was mesmerised by the energy he exuded.

This was Talos stripped back, in all his graceful, powerful glory.

Sweat dripped off him, his muscles rippled, his punches were hard and merciless—as if he were imagining the punching bag as a living target, a foe to be destroyed.

He was in pain. She knew that as surely as she knew her own name. His pain was in every one of his punches.

He must have caught sight of her in the mirror, for he suddenly stopped and spun around. Breathing heavily, he stared at her disbelievingly, his throat moving, his jaw clenched.

Her lips parted to apologise for the intrusion—and it *was* an intrusion—but the words stuck in her throat.

Not taking his eyes off her, Talos reached for a towel and wiped his face and chest, then dropped it to the floor and prowled over to stand before her.

His chest was rising and falling in rapid motion, and his nostrils flared before his mouth came crashing down on hers and she was pushed back against the wall.

His kisses were hungry, the kisses of a starving man. His powerful strength was something she'd always been hugely aware of, but until that moment she'd never appreciated the restraint he displayed around her. Now, holding her upright against the wall with one arm, he gripped her hip with his free hand and pulled her tight against him, before loosening his grip to slide his hand down her thigh to the hem of her short skirt and rip her knickers off. Manipulating her thighs to wrap around him, he freed himself from his shorts and plunged into her with a groan that spoke as much of pain as it did of pleasure.

Amalie held him tight, breathing in his salty, woody scent, cradling his scalp, wanting only to take away his pain.

As far as lovemaking went this was fierce, primal, but she embraced every carnal thrust, felt the pulsations building in her core as she clung to him.

He gave a roar and buried his face in her hair, his whole body shaking, and his final thrust pushed her over the edge as the pulsations exploded with a shocking power that took all the life from her bones and left her limp in his arms.

Time lost any meaning.

It was only when he gently placed her back on her feet, tugged her skirt down from around her waist and stepped back, that she saw the red mark on the top of his shoulder and realised she had made it with her mouth.

Talos spotted it too and gave a ragged grin. 'My first love bite,' he said, in an attempt at humour that didn't fool her for a second.

She waited for him to ask why she was there, but all he did was cup her cheeks and kiss her with something close to desperation, then pull her to him.

'I'm sorry,' he said, his voice husky. 'That was incredibly selfish of me.'

'I'm not,' she murmured, tilting her head to look up at him.

His eyes closed and he muttered an oath. 'I didn't use protection.'

That made her blink. She hadn't been in the right frame of mind to think of protection either.

'We should be okay. I'm due on tomorrow.'

'*Should* be okay?' He gave a savage shake of his head.

'I'm not an expert, but I'm certain I'm way past the ovulation stage of my cycle. And I'm always regular,' she added, trying to reassure him even while the image of a dark-haired baby wrapped in vine leaves filtered into her mind. 'I'll know within a couple of days if we have a problem.'

The pulse in his jaw was working overtime. 'Make sure to tell me the minute you know.'

'I promise.' She hesitated before asking, 'Talos, what's wrong? You've become so distant.'

He gazed back down at her, and for a moment she was certain he was about to talk. Instead, he pulled his arms away and took a step back.

'Nothing's wrong. I'm a little stressed about the gala, I have a few minor problems with work, a lack of sleep…the usual.'

'I'm sure the rehearsals tomorrow will go better,' she said, trying to inject positivity into her tone. 'At least I was able to play it today.'

Even if it *had* sounded like a cats' chorus ringing out, and even if the members of her orchestra *had* been gazing at her with something close to horror.

He raised his eyes to the ceiling and shook his head, before jerking it into a nod. 'I'm sure you're right.'

And in that moment she knew he was lying.

He wasn't merely *concerned*.

He didn't believe she could do it.

Panic took hold in her chest.

Up until that point Talos's conviction that he could fix her had taken root in her head, allowing her to believe that she could overcome her fear in time. But if her warrior prince had lost faith, what did *that* say? Where did that leave her? Where did that leave *them*?

'I need to go to Athens first thing in the morning,' he said, rubbing the back of his neck. 'I'll collect you at seven for dinner with my grandfather.'

Was this his way of dismissing her?

'Okay…' she answered uncertainly. 'Are you certain it's informal dress?'

'My grandfather insists. He wants it to be a relaxed occasion, where you can both talk without formality.'

'That sounds good,' she said. 'Are you coming back to the cottage with me?'

Instinct had already told her his answer, but she had to ask. She wouldn't presume to invite herself to stay here at the villa with him—even if it wasn't so obvious he wished her gone.

'Not tonight. I've an early start. I'll only disturb you if I stay over, and you need a good night's sleep as much as I do. I'll walk you back.'

His words made sense. That didn't stop them feeling like a knife plunging into her heart.

She forced a smile to her face and leaned up to kiss him, pretending that nothing was wrong when it was blindingly obvious that he was steeling himself to end their relationship.

Not that what they shared was a relationship, she scolded herself on their silent walk back to the cottage. It had always had an end date attached to it; she had accepted that. She just hadn't considered that he would tire of her before the end date. She hadn't considered that he would lose faith in her.

Amalie strove to hide the shock that meeting King Astraeus Kalliakis evoked.

With Talos's hand in the small of her back, they had been escorted by a courtier to the King's private dining room—a space a fraction of the size of the Banquet Room but every bit as sumptuous.

The pictures she'd seen of the King had depicted a tall, handsome man. Even at his eightieth birthday celebrations, with his ebony hair having thinned and turned white, he'd exuded vitality. That was the man she had prepared herself to meet.

'Forgive me for not rising to greet you,' he said, his voice weak. 'If I could get up I would kiss your hand.'

She had no idea what possessed her, but when she took the unsteady hand he offered she was the one to place a kiss on the paper-thin skin, rather than giving the curtsy she'd practised earlier.

He smiled warmly, then indicated for his nurse to wheel him to the table.

Amalie tried to catch Talos's eye but he was avoiding her gaze, just as he'd avoided any conversation other than the usual pleasantries on their drive to the palace. He hadn't even mentioned her phone call early that morning confirming that her period had started.

As masochistic as she knew it to be, she'd felt a definite twinge of disappointment when she'd spotted the telltale signs of her period. She'd never even *thought* of having children before. Not once. But for less than twelve hours there had been the smallest of chances that she might have conceived and her imagination had taken root. Any initial concerns about what a disaster it would be, seeing as she was in anything *but* a loving relationship, and it would affect the career she longed to reclaim, had fallen by the wayside as she'd imagined what it would be like to have Talos's child.

It had felt almost dreamlike.

She had no idea if she would be any good as a mother, but instinct told her he would make a fantastic father. She sighed. It was something she would never know, and it was pointless to allow her thoughts to run in such wayward directions, not when there were so many other things occupying her mind.

When she'd given Talos the news his response had been a distant, 'That's one less thing to worry about.'

And now she knew why he'd been so distant. He had been thinking of his grandfather.

Why hadn't he told her his grandfather was ill? And not just ill, but clearly dying. It was there in the gauntness of his features—he must have lost half his body weight since those pictures had been taken at his eightieth. And it was there in the sallow yellow complexion of his skin, the hollowness of his eyes… It was everywhere. She could feel it.

'You must be curious as to why I wanted to meet

you,' the King rasped, once their first course of tomato and basil soup had been served.

'I assumed you wanted to meet the woman who will play your wife's final composition.'

As she spoke, her skin chilled. Today's rehearsal had been a step backwards.

It had started well enough. Christophe, the orchestra's conductor for the gala, had found a screen for her to hide behind, so she could actually play in time with the orchestra. It had worked beautifully. Then the screen had been removed and she'd found herself breathing in and out of a paper bag in an effort to stem the panic attack clawing at her.

Christophe was on the verge of his own nervous breakdown, freaking out so much he'd contracted a hypnotist to fly over to Agon for her.

She'd searched in vain for Talos, waiting for him to step through the practice room's door and give her confidence with a simple smile. But he'd been in Athens. If he was by her side she would be able to get through it; they'd already proved that. With more practice, and with Talos and his calming presence, she might be able to do the score the justice she gave it when they were alone.

'Indeed.' Watery brown eyes held hers. 'Tell me about yourself, *despinis*.'

'My career?'

That would be a very short conversation.

He waved a hand. 'I want to know about *you*. The music you enjoy, the books you read, the films you watch.'

And so they fell into easy conversation, Amalie doing most of the talking and the King making the odd encouraging comment. She was thankful for her childhood spent surrounded by powerful people, otherwise she would have been completely overwhelmed to be dining with a king.

He ate very little: a few spoonfuls of soup…a couple of bites of the main course of red snapper.

Talos stayed silent, following the conversation without contributing, his gaze on his grandfather. He didn't once meet her eyes.

When the dessert was brought in—light pistachio cakes with an accompanying chocolate mousse—the King finally asked her something in connection with the violin.

'Do you find it hard, learning new music?'

She considered the question, aware that Talos was finally looking at her. 'It's like reading a book where the words are notes and all the adjectives are replaced with tempos and dynamics.'

Astraeus gave a wheezy laugh. 'I'm sure that makes sense to you.'

She couldn't help but laugh too. 'I've probably over-complicated it. I should have just said I read music the way you read a book.'

'And how did you find learning my wife's music?'

'I found it the most fulfilling experience of my entire musical life,' she answered with honesty, trying to tune out Talos's stare. 'To know I am the first person to play it publicly... Can I ask you a question?'

The King nodded.

'Did she ever play it for you?'

'No.' His eyes dimmed. 'She never spoke of her music when she was composing. When she finished a piece, only then would she tell me about it and play it for me.' His shoulders slumped. 'She contracted pneumonia shortly before she completed this one. She struggled to finish it, but my wife was a very determined woman. She died two days later.'

'I'm very sorry.'

'I still miss her. All the time.'

Forgetting protocol—not that she even knew what the protocol for an audience with the King *was*, as Talos hadn't seen fit to fill her in—she leaned over and placed her hand on his.

Shock flared in his eyes but he made no effort to relinquish her hold, tilting his frail body a little closer to her.

'What your wife created,' Amalie said gently, 'was a concerto about love. It's a tribute to *you*.'

'How do you know this?' he whispered, leaning even closer.

'It's all there in the music. I can't explain how I know, but I feel it. She wrote this score with love in her heart—not maternal love, but romantic love.'

The King's eyes closed. For a moment she allowed her glance to dart at Talos. He sat rigid, his jaw set, his eyes filled with something she couldn't comprehend.

When Astraeus opened his eyes he stared at her with great concentration, before turning his head to the courtier standing to his right and nodding at him. The courtier left the dining room, returning almost immediately with a violin case. He laid it on the table before the King.

Astraeus gestured for Amalie to open it.

Apprehensive, certain he was going to ask her to play for him, she obeyed. The gorgeous scent of wood and resin puffed out and she inhaled it greedily, as she had done since toddlerhood, when her father would open *his* violin case.

She made to lift the violin out but the King stopped her, placing his hand on the instrument and stroking it.

'This belonged to Rhea,' he said. 'It was hand-crafted for her by Massimo Cinelli. It was my wedding present to her.'

Massimo Cinelli was one of the foremost twentieth-century luthiers, a man who made string instruments of such tonal quality it was argued that they rivalled Stradivarius. His had been a life cut tragically short, and when he'd died at the age of fifty-three he had been known to have made around three hundred string instruments, a quarter of which were violins. In recent months an auction for one of his violas had fetched a value of half a million pounds.

Amalie could only imagine what a violin made for a queen would fetch—especially a queen who'd left such a huge legacy to the classical music world. It made her joyful and sad all at the same time to know this would have been the violin Rhea had used at Carnegie Hall, when she'd played with Amalie's father all those years ago.

'I am bequeathing it to you,' the King said.

'What do you mean?'

Surely he had to be talking about her using it for the gala?

'It is yours, child.'

'Mine...?'

His smile was sad. 'It's sat in darkness for five years. It needs to be played. I know you will treasure it and I know you will honour Rhea's memory. Take it, child—it's yours.'

Amalie was truly lost for words. She knew this was no joke, but all the same... The King of Agon had just given her one of his wife's most prized possessions—a gift beyond value.

'Thank you,' she said, shrugging her shoulders with helplessness at her inability to come up with anything more meaningful.

'No. Thank *you*,' he answered enigmatically, then beckoned his nurse over and spoke to her in Greek.

The nurse took hold of his wheelchair.

'And now I bid you a good night,' Astraeus said. 'It has been a pleasure meeting you, *despinis*.'

'It has been an honour, Your Majesty.'

Talos had risen to his feet, so she followed suit, only to have the King take her hand and tug her down so he could speak in her ear. 'I'm glad my grandson has found you. Please look after him for me when I'm gone.'

In another breach of protocol she kissed his cold cheek and whispered, 'I promise I'll try.'

It was the best she could do. She doubted Talos would ever give her the chance.

CHAPTER FOURTEEN

A DRIVER RETURNED them to Talos's estate. They'd been sitting in the back, the partition up, for a few minutes before he spoke.

'What did my grandfather say to you?'

That was what he was concerned about? Not that she'd been given a family heirloom? The heirloom that now sat on her lap, where she held it tightly.

'I think he whispered it to me because he didn't want you to hear,' she answered, striving for lightness.

'Don't be absurd. I'm his grandson. We have no secrets.'

She finally found the courage to look at him. '*You* hold on to your secrets extremely well. You must have inherited that from somewhere.'

'Are you deliberately talking in riddles?'

'Why didn't you tell me he was ill?'

His jaw set in the clenched fashion it had been fixed in throughout the evening. Her heart ached to see it and she wished she could breach the wall he'd erected between them. Even before they'd become lovers she'd never felt as if she couldn't touch him, but right then she was certain that if she reached out he would recoil from her.

'My grandfather's illness is not a subject for idle gossip.'

'I appreciate that.'

She took a breath. It wasn't so much his answer that had cut, but the dismissive tone in which he'd said it. As if she were no one.

'But if you'd told me the truth about his health from the beginning...'

'Then *what*?' he asked bitingly. 'You would have agreed to perform for him *without* having to be blackmailed into it?'

'I don't know.' She tightened her grip on the violin case, soothing her fingers on the velvety material. It was the only part of her she could soothe. 'I don't know if things would have been different— my point is you never gave me the chance to find out if I would have reacted differently.'

'You wouldn't have,' he said, with tight assurance.

'We'll never know.' Now she clenched her own teeth, before loosening them. 'What I don't understand is why you haven't told me since. We've shared a bed for over a fortnight.'

There had been plenty of opportunities for him to tell her. Times when she'd asked him if there was something wrong. The time she'd asked him outright if the gala held more importance to him than the reason he'd shared with her.

'Do not presume that sharing a bed means I owe you anything.'

She had never known him to be this cold. She'd never known him to be cold at all. When something angered him Talos *burned*.

This coldness chilled her to the bone.

The car came to a stop. The driver opened her door.

Not another word was exchanged as she got out and entered the cottage. Not a word of goodnight. Not a kiss. Not a touch. Not a look.

She flinched to hear the engine spark back to life and the car driving off, taking Talos to his villa.

Feeling as if lead weights had been inserted into her limbs, she kicked off her shoes and placed Rhea Kalliakis's violin on the piano. If she didn't feel so numb she would already have it out of the case and be tuning it. This was a *Cinelli*. Any other violinist in the world would likely have passed out with shock to be given it. It was the classical violinist's version of winning the lottery.

But the weight of the gift lay heavily on her. And Talos's parting words lay even heavier.

'Do not presume that sharing a bed means I owe you anything.'

He'd really said that. He'd hardly said a word all night but he'd said *that*. And as the full weight of those words filtered through her brain the numbness disappeared, pain lanced through her, and something even more powerful filled her.

Anger. Unadulterated rage.

How *dared* he talk to her as if she were nothing more than a notch on his bedpost?

Consumed with a fury she only partly understood, she flung open the front door and ran out into the night. Cutting through the trees, she saw the lights of the villa in the distance, along with the lights of the car just approaching it.

The lead in her limbs had gone. Her legs were now seemingly made of air as she flew over the fields, running faster than she'd ever known she could, the wind rippling against her face, the skirt of her blue summer dress billowing out behind her.

It seemed as if no time had passed before she set the security lights ablaze. In the time it had taken her to race there the car had dropped Talos off and begun its return journey to the palace.

As she banged on the front door with her fist, then punched the doorbell, she was assailed with memories of that morning a month before, when Talos had knocked on her own front door and turned her world on its axis.

The door was wrenched open.

Talos stood there, staring at her as if she'd just appeared from the moon.

'Sharing your bed doesn't mean I *presume* you owe me anything—let alone know what's going on in your head,' she spat from her place on the doorstep, before he could utter a word. 'But we've shared more than just a bed. Or at least *I* have.'

He looked murderous. He looked as if he wanted nothing more than to wrap his hands around her throat.

'Have you run all the way here from the cottage *in the dark*? Are you *insane*? It's the middle of the night—there could be anyone out there!'

'You didn't worry about that the other night when I walked here in the dark.'

Suddenly the exertion of her run hit her and she bent over, grabbing her knees as she fought desperately to breathe. God, but her lungs burned.

'Amalie?'

She lifted her head to look at him, puffing in air until she felt able to straighten again.

He stared at her with eyes now curiously vacant. His detachment ratcheted her fury up another notch.

She straightened. 'Do not treat me as if I'm some nothing you had sex with just because it was available. It was more than that and you know it—and you owe me more than to treat me like that.'

'I do not owe you anything. If you think your being a virgin before we became lovers means I have to treat you—'

'It's nothing to do with me being a virgin!' she yelled, punching him in the shoulder.

He didn't so much as jolt.

'This is to do with me sharing everything with you. I spilled my guts about my childhood and my life to you. I gave you *everything*! I didn't expect a marriage proposal, or declarations of love, but I *did* expect some respect.'

'It was never my intention to be disrespectful.'

'Then what *was* your intention? Tell me, damn you. Why have you closed yourself off? I thought you were frustrated because I'm still struggling to play with the orchestra, but now I'm wondering if you're just bored with me. Is that it? Are you too gutless to tell me that you don't want me any more and rather than come out and say it you're taking the coward's way of withdrawing, hoping I'll get the hint?'

Her voice had risen to a shout. No doubt half the live-in staff had been woken.

Suddenly he jerked forward and grabbed her forearm. 'Come with me,' he said through gritted teeth, marching her through the reception room, down a wide corridor and through a door that revealed what at first glance appeared to be an office, filled with plush masculine furniture.

He slammed the door shut and loomed over her, his arms folded over his chest. His eyes had darkened to a point of blackness.

'First of all, do *not* presume to tell me what I think.'

'I have to make assumptions because you don't tell me anything!'

'What do you want me to say? Do you want me to *apologise* because my grandfather is dying?'

'No!' She clamped her teeth together and blinked back the sudden stinging tears welling in the backs of her eyes. 'Of course not. I didn't mean—'

Before she knew what was happening Talos's control shattered before her eyes.

He punched the wall, blackness seeping out of him. 'I know what you meant. You think because you have shared confidences with me that I must do the same in return.'

'No!' She shook her head over and over, terrified not for herself but for him. She'd never seen such pain before, etched on every line of his face and in every movement of his powerful body.

He seemed not to hear her, kicking the solid wood desk with such force he put a dent in it. 'Do you want me to pour my heart out about my childhood? To understand where my nightmares come from and why I went so off the rails in my adolescence? Is that what you want?'

'I—'

'Do you want to hear about the day I watched my father punch my mother not once but a dozen times in the stomach? Do you want to hear how I jumped on his back to protect her and how he threw me off with such force my head split open on their bedframe? That my lasting memory of my mother is her holding me and her tears falling on my bleeding head? Is *that* what you want? To know that I couldn't protect her then and that my vow to always protect her in the future came to nothing, because two hours later both my parents were dead? And now my grandfather is dying too. And I have to accept that as a fact of life and accept there is nothing I can do about it. You want me to share how I feel? Well, it feels as if my stomach and heart have been shredded into nothing. Is that enough for you? Is that what you wanted to hear?'

His eyes suddenly found hers, and he threw his hands in the air and stalked towards her.

'So now you know all my dirty little secrets and I know yours, is there anything else you want from me or feel I should tell you, seeing as we're having such a *wonderful* time trading confidences?'

If it hadn't been for the wildness radiating from his eyes she would have hated him for his contempt. But she couldn't. All she felt was horror.

'No?' He leaned down so his face was right against hers. 'In that case, seeing as you've got what you wanted from me, you can leave.'

Abruptly he turned away and lifted the phone on the sprawling desk, rasping words in Greek to whoever was on the receiving end.

'Talos…' she said hesitantly when he'd replaced the receiver.

She didn't know what she wanted to say. Couldn't

think of anything *to* say. What she did want was to take him in her arms and hold him close, but she knew without having to be told he didn't want that. He didn't want her or the solace she yearned to give him.

'We have nothing more to say to each other.' He seemed to have regained his composure, but his focus on her was stark. 'We've enjoyed each other's company but this is as far as we go.'

A knock on the door made her start.

Talos pulled it open and indicated for her to leave. 'Kostas will take you back to the cottage. I hope for everyone's sake the hypnotist your conductor has arranged for you works, because there is nothing more *I* can do to help you.'

With as much dignity as she could summon Amalie walked past him to Kostas, who had already set off to the front door.

Talos kicked the covers off and got out of bed. A large glass of single malt should help him sleep.

He glanced out of the window. Three o'clock in the morning and all was in darkness, but in the downward sloping distance he could see the dim lights of the cottage.

Amalie was awake.

He closed his eyes. He would bet every last cent he owned that at that very minute she was playing his grandmother's violin, taking the only comfort she could. In his mind's eye he watched her fingers flying over the strings, imagined the purity of the sound she produced. Knew that to hear it would tear his soul in half. That was if any part of his soul remained. After the way he'd spoken to her the other night whatever had been left of it had been ripped out.

He'd treated her abominably. He still didn't know where all that rage had come from, knew only that she'd been getting too close. He'd been trying to protect himself. Squashing anything that resembled an emotion down into a tight little ball that could be hidden away and forgotten about.

Somehow Amalie had unpicked the edges of that ball and it had exploded back into life, making him feel more than a man could bear.

Theos, had he ever felt more wretched?

He'd been heartsick before—of course he had; the loss of his parents had devastated him. His father had been a brute, but Talos had still loved him…with the blind faith with which all small children loved their parents.

This felt different, as if the weight of a thousand

bass drums had compressed inside him, beating their solemn sound through his aching bones.

He was wasted, physically and emotionally.

He closed his eyes, imagined Amalie padding into his room and settling on the corner of his bed to play for him, her music soothing him enough to drive all the demons from his head.

He hadn't known his grandfather intended to give her the violin, but he couldn't think of a better person to have it. What good would it do sitting in a glass cabinet in the Kalliakis palace museum, nothing but a tourist attraction? At least Amalie would love and care for it. When she played it she would play with her heart.

He'd spent the day deliberately avoiding anyone connected with the orchestra. But palace whispers ran more quickly than the tide, and his avoidance hadn't stopped rumours about the solo violinist having to play behind a screen for the third day in a row reaching his ears.

He imagined her standing there, shaking, her face white and pinched, terror in those beautiful green eyes, her breath coming in increasingly shallow jerks.

What was he *doing* to her?

It would be kinder to strip her naked and stand her on display. The humiliation would be less.

She'd come so far—been so incredibly brave. To force her to go ahead with the gala now would surely ensure his damnation to hell. Forget any potential ruination of the gala—forcing Amalie to go ahead would completely destroy her.

He couldn't do it to her.

He would rather rip his own heart out than let her suffer any more.

Amalie rubbed her sleep-deprived eyes, then picked up her knife and chopped the melon into small chunks, the action making her think of Talos and the knife he carried everywhere with him.

Do not think of him, she ordered herself. *Not today.*

There would be plenty of time to mourn what had happened between them when she returned to Paris, but for now she had to get through today. That was all she should focus on.

The scent of the melon was as fragrant as all the fruit she'd had since her arrival on the island, but her stomach stubbornly refused to react to it other than to gurgle with nausea.

Please, stomach, she begged, *accept some form of nourishment.*

At the rate she was going, even if she managed to get on to the outdoor stage that evening, she would likely fall into a faint when the heat of the spotlight fell upon her and her starved belly reacted to it.

Hearing movement, she cut through to the entrance hall and found a letter had been pushed through the door.

A heavy cream-coloured A4 envelope with *'Amalie Cartwright'* written on it with a penmanship that resembled a slash.

Her heart thundering erratically, it was clear her body knew who the sender was before she'd torn it open.

In the top right-hand corner was Talos's full name, including his royal title and the palace address.

Dear Mademoiselle Cartwright

This letter is written to confirm the cancellation of the contract between us dated tenth March. All penalties stipulated in the contract are hereby revoked, and the Orchestre National de Paris shall continue in its current form.

Sincerely,

Talos Kalliakis

Her head swimming, Amalie read it a number of times before the words sank in.

Her stomach dived, nausea clutching her throat.

One hand over her mouth, the other pressed against her heavy, thundering heart, she swayed into a table, fighting to stop the deluge of misery knocking her from her feet.

He didn't believe she could do it.

He really had given up on her.

It was over.

Everything.

His belief in her.

Her reignited dreams of playing on a stage.

All gone.

But before the despair could crush her in its entirety, a thought struck her.

Why now, on the day of the gala—the day they'd spent a month preparing for...?

She rubbed her eyes, frantically trying to stem the tears pouring out of them, and read it one more time.

It didn't make any sense.

She looked at her watch. Nine a.m. The gala would be starting in six hours. She was due on-stage to perform the solo and close the gala in eleven hours. The schedule had been released to the media, who were crawling all over the island in preparation for the day's events. At that moment heads of state were preparing to descend on the island.

And Talos was allowing her to leave.

No, it really did not make any sense.

Since their last encounter she'd done nothing but think of him and his words. She'd known from the beginning that her playing his grandmother's final composition was important to him—you didn't blackmail and threaten someone for something trivial. Dining with his grandfather had brought the true importance of the gala to life for her. This was King Astraeus's swansong. This was the final celebration of his life.

And now Talos was prepared to scrap what he'd fought so hard to attain.

His grandparents had raised him and his brothers since he was seven. His family meant everything to him. This piece of music meant everything to his entire family. Of all the things the gala represented, *this* was the performance that meant the most. It wasn't just the icing on the cake; it was the sponge and filling too.

She thought back to that evening three days ago, and the contempt in his voice when he'd ordered her to leave his villa. She'd thought then that the contempt was directed at *her*, but suddenly she realised it had been directed inwards, at himself.

And suddenly she realised something else.

For Talos to release her from the contract now meant he was putting her emotional well-being above *everything*.

Talos Kalliakis was a warrior. He would fight to the bitter end, even if it meant frogmarching her onto the stage and holding her upright while she played. Their time together had proved she could play when she was with him—something he would use as a weapon in his arsenal He would carry on their affair until she'd outlived her use. He wouldn't have lost faith in her because faith didn't exist in his vocabulary. For Talos it was all about spirit and belief.

She thought back to the rehearsal earlier in the week, when his presence had enabled her to play the whole piece without having to hide behind a screen. There had been pride in his brown eyes, but mingled with it had been something troubled. Now she understood what that had meant—her distress had troubled him on a *personal* level.

She scrambled for her phone and scrolled through

her contacts until she found the gala coordinator's name. She pressed the call button.

'Has the schedule been changed?' Amalie asked without preamble.

'I was told an hour ago that the final orchestral piece has been changed,' the coordinator replied. 'I'm still waiting to hear what it's been changed *to*.'

'But my orchestra will still be performing the final piece?'

'Yes.'

'Thank you.'

Disconnecting the call, Amalie rubbed a hand over her mouth, then dialled Melina's number. The kickboxing instructor's *froideur* towards her had thawed over time—enough so that she'd given Amalie her number.

'Melina? I need your help...'

CHAPTER FIFTEEN

THE GALA WAS proving to be a huge success. The open-air theatre was filled; not a single seat was free. The day had started with Helios announcing his engagement to Princess Catalina of Monte Cleure, and then the guests had been treated to a variety of acts—from a children's choir to a world-famous circus troupe—and each in turn had been given rapturous applause.

Talos was too keyed up to enjoy it.

He'd sat down with his grandfather that morning and explained that Amalie would not be performing after all. He'd told him that the orchestra had rehearsed in Paris with another violinist before flying over, and how that violinist was prepared to take the role.

His grandfather had looked him straight in the eye and replied, 'An understudy won't do. We both know Amalie is the one.'

Talos had responded with a sharp nod, refusing to

think of the undertone in his grandfather's words or the expression in his eyes as he'd said them.

The penultimate act was on stage now; Agon's Royal Ballet School, performing a condensed version of the *Nutcracker Suite* with the accompaniment of Agon's Royal Orchestra. Ballet bored him at the best of times, but tonight he didn't notice a single thing about it. As hard as he tried to concentrate, his mind was with Amalie.

His grandfather, sitting to his left with a blanket snug over his lap, was thoroughly enjoying it all, nodding along to the more upbeat performances and snoozing his way through those that failed to capture his attention.

If Helios and his new fiancée were enjoying it they were doing a fine job of pretending otherwise, the atmosphere between them decidedly frosty. And Theseus… He might as well not be there, for all the attention he was paying to the acts.

Finally the ballet finished and the curtains closed so that the Orchestre National de Paris could set up with privacy. Talos could not care less what piece they chose to play as a replacement. His only stipulation was that it must not be the 'Méditation' from *Thaïs*.

The compère, a famous American comedian,

came onstage and told some jokes to keep the crowd entertained. They'd been sitting in the amphitheatre for over five hours but showed no sign of restlessness.

The audience burst into a roar of laughter at a joke the compère had told but Talos hadn't heard a word of it.

Grinning hugely, the compère pressed a finger to his ear, listening to his earpiece, then raised a hand for silence.

'It is now time for the final performance,' he said, becoming solemn. 'As this is such a special occasion only the most special performance can be allowed to finish it. Ladies and gentlemen, performing the final composition of this beautiful island's Queen Rhea, I give you the Orchestre National de Paris and their celebrated violinist, Amalie Cartwright.'

What...?

Loud applause broke out, and the curtains were drawn back to reveal the orchestra already seated.

Heart thumping, Talos's first thought was that someone had forgotten to tell the compère about the change. It had been too late to alter the programmes, so they'd agreed that the compère would inform the audience that Amalie had been taken ill.

He got to his feet, ready to find out what had gone wrong.

Then he spotted the figure standing at the front left-hand side of the stage.

His heart twisted into a clenched fist. He couldn't move; his feet seemed rooted to the floor until his grandfather took hold of his wrist and gently tugged it.

Unable to move his eyes away from her, he sat back down, breathing heavily.

Amalie looked beautiful. Divine. She wore a snug-fitting mid-thigh-length dress, with a scooped neckline and short sleeves. Its red wine colour set her apart from her orchestra, who all wore black. It highlighted the paleness of her skin, and with her hair swept up in an elegant knot she looked fragile. Incredibly fragile. And scared—like the rabbit caught in the headlights he'd found in the Parisian practice room all those long weeks ago.

Her eyes searched his side of the crowd until she found the royal box. It was too dark for her to pick him out but he swore that she found him.

The conductor stood before the orchestra and silence fell. The first pluck from the string section echoed out, then the whisper of the flutes.

Amalie's teeth bit into her lip before she placed

her violin under her chin and put her bow in position. She straightened, visibly strengthening. Then she closed her eyes, listened for her cue and played the first note.

Talos held his breath. Beside him, he heard his brothers and grandfather hold their breaths too. It had been an open secret around the palace that the star soloist was suffering from a severe case of stage fright.

Their worry was unfounded.

Her eyes scrunched tightly shut, Amalie began to play.

When she'd played the piece for him in the bedroom the beauty of the underlying melody had made his heart expand. Coupled with the accompanying orchestral arrangement it was taken to a whole new level of beauty, heightening the sensation he'd experienced that first time, pulling him into a swell of emotion.

Watching her, the sway of her hips as she played with the whole of her body, the marvel of her finger-work, the purity of her vibrato…

The child prodigy was reborn—a virtuoso of such melodic stature that he was certain there couldn't be a dry eye in the amphitheatre.

As she approached the climax of the piece—the

part that tore his heart into shreds—her eyes flew open and found the royal box. She was crying, he realised, huge tears falling down her cheeks.

His grandfather tugged at his sleeve for attention.

Blinking away the burn at the back of his eyes, Talos felt his chest constrict to see his grandfather's face also swimming with tears.

'Surely my fighter of a grandson isn't so scared of a woman's love that he would throw away his one chance of true happiness?' he asked in a choked voice.

It was as if his grandfather had stared right into his heart and read what was there. And in that moment the truth hit him with full force.

Suddenly it was there, as if he'd always known. There in his head. In his heart.

He'd fallen in love with her.

As epiphanies went, it beat them all.

He loved her.

Gazing back at the beautiful woman who held the thousands in the audience in silent captivation, he had never felt so full; as if his heart and chest had expanded so much they could explode out of him.

Theos, she was magnificent…holding her composure right until the final note played out.

The applause was instantaneous.

Everybody got to their feet, orchestra and crowd alike.

Wiping her face with shaking hands, Amalie bowed to the royal box, then bowed again to the audience at large. The conductor strode over to her, clapping hard, then put his hands on her shoulders and kissed her cheeks, then bowed to her. She laughed and put a hand over her mouth, so clearly overwhelmed at the reaction that Talos wanted to run on to the stage and scoop her into his arms.

But this was her moment, and she needed to cherish it.

She found the royal box again, kissed her hand, then pointed it at his grandfather, more tears falling down her cheeks.

The crowd were calling for an encore.

Amalie, the rest of the Orchestre National de Paris and all the other performers were whisked back inside the palace for the after-gala do.

She took the offered champagne and drank it with gratitude, still dazed at what she had accomplished.

She had done it.

Her parents had both messaged her.

Her father's message had read: I'm very proud of you, sweetheart—maybe the old dream of playing together at Carnegie Hall might one day come true xxx, while her mother's had been much longer and more rambling, but filled with just as much pride.

On impulse, she'd messaged them both back, suggesting the two of them celebrate together. Life was too short to be miserable, and far too short to be alone. They'd been divorced from each other almost as long as they'd been married, and still neither of them was happy without the other. If there was one thing Amalie had learned during her time on Agon it was that it was time to forgive the past. They needed to forgive it too.

A gong rang out, which brought everyone in the ballroom to attention. A courtier entered the room and announced the arrival of His Majesty King Astraeus and the Princes Helios, Theseus and Talos.

Her stomach somersaulted as a different courtier approached to lead her over to the royal family. She'd been warned that she would be the first one to be addressed by them.

Taking a deep breath, she finished her champagne and followed him to where the royal family were lined up, awaiting her. The other guests were forming an orderly queue, and she was taken to the head of it.

The King, frail in his wheelchair, broke into a smile to see her and grabbed her hands with surprising strength to tug her down to him. A tear trailed down his cheek. 'Thank you, *despinis*. Thank you from the bottom of my heart.'

Her own eyes filled. Hadn't she cried enough for one evening? Having not cried in years, her life being too safe for anything emotional to pierce her, it was as if her tear ducts were now making up for it.

'It was an honour,' she whispered.

This time it was the King who breached protocol, planting a kiss to her cheek, and then he indicated for his nurse to wheel him out, leaving the queue of people behind her staring in disbelief as the King left his own party.

Theseus was next in line, and surprised her by ignoring her hand and clumsy curtsy to kiss her on both cheeks. His eyes were a darker brown than Talos's, and rang with a strong emotion he didn't have to put into words.

Helios was even more demonstrative, pulling her into his arms for a tight embrace and whispering in her ear, 'My family honours you—our island is your home for as long as you want it to be.'

And then it was Talos's turn.

Jaw clenched, he shook her hand formally—his own had a bandage wrapped tightly around its forefinger and index finger—and bowed as she made her curtsy.

She met his eyes. 'You've hurt your hand…' She thought back to the punch he'd given the wall of his office, and to the time she'd found him thumping that punching bag without protective gloves on.

'It'll heal.' A pulse throbbed beneath his ear, the black pupils of his eyes thick and dilating as he gazed at her without speaking any further.

She didn't know what to say. She knew he cared for her, but that didn't mean anything had changed. No matter how his feelings for her had developed, it didn't change the fact that he was a lone wolf.

Did lone wolves ever pair up?

Aware of the other performers jostling next to her, eager to have their audience with him, she turned to walk away but a huge arm hooked around her waist.

'Where do you think you're going?' he said roughly, pulling her away from the line.

Joy filled her so rapidly she felt her toes lifting

with the extra air it generated. 'I was letting the others have their audience with you.'

'I don't want an audience with anyone but you.' He steered her further away from the line approaching the Princes, now a good two hundred people deep.

'Shouldn't you stay with your brothers?'

His massive shoulders lifted into a nonchalant shrug. 'They can handle it.'

She couldn't prevent the smile that broadened across her face so widely she felt it pull at every muscle in her face.

Talos wanted privacy for them. This was not a conversation he wanted to have with his brothers and hundreds of guests watching.

Gripping her hand firmly, he steered her out of the ballroom and through all the corridors they'd travelled together three weeks before. He hadn't expected her to agree so readily to his request to talk. After the way he'd spoken to her the other night he hadn't expected much more from her than a possible slap around the face.

He also hadn't expected that she would hold his hand as tightly as he held hers—so tightly it was as if she didn't want to let it go...

Punching in the security code for his private

apartment, he led her inside. Dropping his hold on her hand, he strode to the high window of his living area, braced himself, and then turned around to face her properly.

'Before I say anything further I need to apologise for forcing you to come here to my island. The contract I made you sign and the pressure I put you under was unforgivable.'

She smiled. 'Thank you.'

What was she smiling for? 'There is no excuse.'

'Maybe not, but I forgave you ages ago.'

'I treated you abysmally. I refused to take you or your fears seriously because I am an arrogant bastard who thinks only of himself.'

'The arrogant bit is true...' She nodded, her eyes ringing with what looked startlingly like compassion. 'But the rest of your self-assessment is wrong. If you had blackmailed me for your own needs I would never have forgiven you, but it wasn't for selfish reasons. You did it for your grandfather... because you love him.'

He sucked in a breath and swallowed. 'I must also apologise for the way I spoke to you the other night. I lashed out at you, which is also unforgivable.'

'You were in pain.' She closed the gap he'd created between them and placed her hand on his arm. 'I should never have forced the issue with you.'

How could she keep forgiving him and making excuses? He didn't deserve it. He didn't deserve *her*.

'You were right to force it. You were right that what we shared was more than sex. But I was in denial. I lashed out because I find it hard to talk about how I feel, and at the time I was struggling to understand how I felt.'

Those compassionate green eyes held steady on his. 'And how do you feel now?'

How to put into words what was in his heart? He didn't know—knew only that he must.

He took a deep breath.

'All my life I have tried to protect those I…I feel deeply for. I wanted to protect my mother from my father. The night they died I heard them argue. My mother had discovered he was having another affair. She begged him to end it.'

He took another breath.

'My father was an only child and very spoiled. He was never denied anything he wanted. Their marriage was arranged and he wanted it to be one of duty, not love and to be able to continue having his needs met by whatever woman took his eye.

But my mother loved him despite all his faults and couldn't accept that. Whenever she found evidence of his affairs her jealousy would get the better of her. That night their argument escalated and he turned on her with his fists—just as I had heard him do before. This time I summoned up the courage to try and protect her, but I was too small and clumsy. I made a vow to myself that from that moment I would do everything I could to protect her, but I never got the chance.'

Talos stared at the woman he knew he had to open himself to if he had any chance of winning her love. Her eyes were tugged down into crinkles at the corners, her teeth gnawing at her lips, but she kept her silence, letting him speak of the demons in his heart.

'You're the only woman I've met who brings that same compulsion out in me. I wanted to protect you—no, I *want* to protect you. Always.'

'Is that why you released me from the contract?' she asked softly.

'Yes.'

Remembering how magnificently she'd played made him shake his head in awe. Never mind that she'd played as if she were a *Mousai*, a Muse, one of those beautiful goddesses of music and song—

she'd displayed the greatest act of bravery he'd ever witnessed in his life.

'I knew you could do it—believe that—but I couldn't put you through the emotional damage it would bring. Your distress…it cuts me.' He shook his head again. 'How did you get up on that stage?'

'I got Melina to come to the palace and put me through the workout of my life. With all those endorphins racing through my blood I imagined I was an Agonite—a born warrior. I imagined your voice in my head, telling me to fight.'

'But *why*? I gave you a free pass to leave.'

'And it was that freedom which gave me the choice. Do you remember what you said to me? You told me to loosen my hold and fly, and you were right—and the only person who could cut that hold was me. I *wanted* to fly. I *wanted* to throw off the past, stand on that stage and play that beautiful score. And I wanted to do it for you and your grandfather as much as I wanted to do it for me.'

'You wanted to do it for *me*?' How he had hoped…

'I knew how much it meant to you and how much you love your grandmother.'

A painful lump formed in his throat. 'My grandmother died without ever hearing me say those words. When my parents died I became lost, out of control. I didn't want to let people get close to me—not on an emotional level. I have friends... I've had lovers...but I kept them all at an emotional distance. And then you...'

'Me?' she prompted gently, her fingers digging into his arms.

'You...' He swallowed. 'I let you in. I had no choice in it. You crept into my heart.'

Something sparked in her eyes. 'Say it,' she urged. 'Please. Even if you only say it once I won't care, once will be enough. *Say it.*'

'I...'

'Shall I say it first?' Reaching up to palm his face with her hand, she stepped flush against him. 'I love you. You're ferocious and loyal and you've taught me to fly. I will love you until I take my dying breath.'

All the air rushed from his lungs.

'Say it,' she beseeched.

'I love you.' And as he said the words more tumbled out with them. 'I love you and I want to protect and honour you until I take my dying breath.' He kissed her hard. 'I love you.'

Raining kisses all over her face and neck, he

kept repeating those words, letting them sink into every part of him until he was enveloped in the love that bound them so tightly he knew it would never let them go.

'Will you let me love and worship you for ever?' he asked, his hands buried in her silky hair.

'Only if you let me love and worship *you* for ever too.'

'If we marry you'll have no choice. Divorce is forbidden for me, remember…?' He pulled back to look deep into her eyes. '*Will* you marry me?'

'It's only a piece of paper, but I'll sign my heart on it because it belongs to you now. I'm trusting you to take care of it for me.'

'I'll protect it with my life.'

And with those words his hungry mouth moulded to hers.

He felt cleansed. Whole. Loved.

He loved her. And she loved him.

He would say the words to her every day for the rest of his life.

EPILOGUE

AMALIE STEPPED ONTO the sunny balcony of the New York hotel in time to catch Talos hastily turning the page of the newspaper he was reading.

'Stop reading my reviews,' she chided him, settling herself gently onto his lap and nuzzling his neck. Even after two years of marriage she liked nothing more than to bury herself into him and smell his gorgeous, woody scent.

He laughed. 'Do you want me to tell you what it says?'

'No.'

It was a standing joke between them.

Talos trawled the media for any review and snippet about her career he could find, getting any paper versions couriered to wherever they happened to be in the world. Although his pride in her touched her deeply, she preferred to live in blissful ignorance of the critics' voices.

The past couple of years had been a whirl. It

made her dizzy to think back on it. After the gala she'd been inundated with offers to perform and record all over the world. Talos had encouraged her to follow her dreams, had been by her side every step of the way. It had been hard—especially the live performing side, which she chose selectively—but the nerves she'd lived with for so long had almost been banished. *Almost.*

He placed a hand to her swollen belly. 'Did you manage to get any sleep?'

'Some.' She kissed his neck. 'Junior gave up playing football in my belly when the sun came up.'

Seven months pregnant with their first child, she already resembled a watermelon. It was a look Talos assured her suited her. She was so excited about the pregnancy she wouldn't have cared if she looked like a bus.

'And how are you feeling about tonight?'

'Sick! But excited too,' she hastened to add.

Being so heavily pregnant meant that she couldn't do the vigorous kickboxing workout that usually served her so well before a performance. And tonight would be the performance she'd spent her whole life waiting for.

Tonight she and her father would be performing onstage together at Carnegie Hall.

'As long as you're there I'll be fine.'

He rubbed a big hand over her back. 'I want you to be more than fine—I want you to enjoy it.'

'Seeing as this is likely my last performance for a very long time, I intend to make the most of every moment.'

He'd started to say something—no doubt about to offer more reassurance—when the suite's buzzer went off.

Talos groaned. 'I bet that's your mother.'

Amalie's parents, who had remarried to great fanfare six months after Amalie and Talos's own nuptials, were staying in the same hotel. Her mother was enjoying the trip enormously, dragging her husband here, there and everywhere as she threw her weight around.

'Let's pretend we're not in,' Amalie murmured.

'She has unnatural senses.'

'We'll pretend to be asleep.'

Grinning, she slipped a hand down to the waistband of his shorts and undid the button.

'Come on, my Prince, take me to bed.'

Brown eyes gleaming, he pressed a kiss to her neck. 'Nothing would give me greater pleasure.'

Smothering their laughter, in case Colette had her ear to the door, they tiptoed into the master bedroom of their suite, sneaked under the bedcovers and pretended to be asleep for a very long time.

* * * * *

If you enjoyed this book, look out for
the next instalment of
THE KALLIAKIS CROWN *trilogy:*

THESEUS DISCOVERS HIS HEIR
Coming next month.

And look out for the concluding story:

HELIOS CROWNS HIS MISTRESS
Coming in June.